The Trail of the

The Tr



First published in eBook and paperback
2024

Contents

# AUTHORS NOTE

Wyatt Steele's great grand pappy came from Dublin. A writer by trade, Declan Kelly had worked on the Irish Times and the so-called Freeman's Journal, reporting on politics and social injustice. In the late 1880's he crossed the Atlantic, arriving in New York he secured work with the Herald Newspaper. The newspaper regularly carried sensational stories, and so Declan headed out West to find some new material for the Herald.

During his travels Declan met many people, and he recorded their lives in his diaries. These are not tales of the old West; these are the firsthand reports from those involved of what happened. Most of the details in the diaries never made it into print. The diaries were passed to my father's father, then to my father and then about ten years ago to me. I'd heard some of the tales they included recounted to me by my father and grandfather in years gone past, but reading them again, and finding new stories of the lives of those long since gone, of the hardship they endured made me want to share these with those interested in this time period. This is the first, and hopefully not the last, of the stories from my grand pappy's diaries. The people you will read about in the following pages existed, the struggles they endured very real, this is not a work of fiction but a recount of an incident in their lives that shaped them.

This book is written in the style of the classic western, but remember, as you turn the pages that the events happened, they are based on the recollections of those who survived. The hopes, dreams, pain and fear were once felt by these people in a very real sense. Their experiences were written down when the events were fresh in their minds and their nerves still raw from what had just happened. Declan frustratingly only ever referred to those he wrote about by their initials. In this tale we have L, N, RC, V and TM. These have become for this fictional re-write - Lucy, Nash, Red Cartwright, Vardy and Ted Murphy.

Enjoy the real West.

# INTRODUCTION

In the dusty town of Green Hollow, where the sun hung low and the shadows stretched long, a lone gunslinger named Red Cartwright strode through the swinging doors of the Five Dice Saloon. His reputation as a peacekeeper had earned him a wary respect among the townsfolk, who knew he could outdraw anyone who dared to disrupt the fragile calm. It was known he'd ridden with the McKiddery gang, a group of Texas rangers who weren't always on the right side of the law. Plus, no-one trusted a half-breed, and Red made no secret of his Apache heritage.

It was easy enough.

His reputation as a man who'd shoot and ask questions later, kept most of the patrons in line, and those filled with whiskey fueled bravado who were fool enough to challenge Red, soon found they'd been out drawn. While their hands were still reaching for their pieces, they'd find themselves staring into the end of the cold barrel of a .44.

It was enough to cause a change of heart. And he looked the part. McKiddery's dollars had provided a tailored black duster coat, beneath which he wore a snug burgundy waistcoat, smart clean white shirt and a silver buckled gun belt, fine lined dark pants fell to rest on shining soft leather boots.

What was in it for Red?

A free bed above the saloon, food and Isiah paid him enough to keep his pocket filled with dollars. The Five Dice Saloon was popular, men came there because it was safe and had the added draw, that, should they dare, they could sit at the poker table with Red Cartwright.

He didn't win every game. If he did none of the town's folk would come back and change their luck. So, he lost occasionally, and gracefully – but on the whole he won – a lot.

Tonight, the saloon was alive with the raucous sounds of laughter and the clinking of glasses. Nothing unusual, it was the normal noise of the evenings in the Five Dice. Red was sitting in his usual chair at the poker table, back to the wall and facing the door. At the table with him was Richy Morris, the town's saddle-maker and Brent Clarkson who owned the Black Spur Ranch just outside of Green Hollow.

Brent had a rugged practical demeanor, shaped by years of hard labor under an unforgiving sun. He wore a wide-brimmed Stetson hat, designed to shield his face from the relentless sun, it was now tipped back on his head revealing sun-bleached and tousled hair that peeked out from beneath the brim. He wore common sense ranchers' clothes, a sturdy flannel shirt with a leather vest, the sleeves now rolled up, revealing thick corded forearms and the hands that held the cards were calloused from work.

Richy, on the other hand, was altogether different, his hair, slicked back and neat, as was his well-groomed moustache. He wore an expensive tailored dark, charcoal suit, the lapels sharp, and his whole person from polished boots to pocket watch to his gold rimmed glasses that were free of dust was in complete contrast to Brent who seemed to leak the dust of the plains.

Red had just lost the last game.

Richy, shaking his head and smiling, reached for the coins and slid them towards himself. "Well, I'll be. 'bout time my luck changed."

"Another?" Red asked amiably, raising his cold blue eyes and meeting those of Richy. He wouldn't be losing the next game, that was for sure.

The saloon doors opened unevenly, the left one swinging back heavily, the other opening only halfway. From between them emerged Sheriff Braddock who made his way towards the bar.

Richy shook his head, his eyes on the back of the Sheriff's head. "No doubt he's in here spending Ted Denver's money."

"Denver?" Brent questioned, glancing over in the sheriff's direction, a frown on his face.

Richy leaned across the table and said confidentially. "Word is Denver paid him to look the other way regarding them cattle he rounded up last week. Everyone knows they belonged to old man Taite. Denver butchered the brands to match his own, and our sheriff is not wanting to see the truth of the matter."

Brent shook his head. "Money speaks loudest in this town, isn't that right?"

Red didn't comment but pulled the cards together. He liked Braddock well enough, the old sheriff even played poker with him on occasion, as he dealt the cards he watched Braddock down another whiskey.

As the evening wore on, Red caught snippets of conversation that hinted at Braddock's reckless behavior. Dan McGraw, one of Red Hollow's more notorious men came in, McGraw was never far from trouble. He shook Braddock's hand, and after the handshake was over, Braddock, smiling, tucked something away inside a pocket on his vest.

Money.

Whispers of him taking bribes from the local outlaws, turning a blind eye to their misdeeds seemed true. Braddock shouldn't be seen propping up a bar next to McGraw let alone sharing a bottle of whiskey with the man.

Red turned his attention back to his companions and his game. Three rounds later, and just as Red was lifting his head to empty his whiskey glass, old man Taite entered.

"This is going to be mighty interesting, fella's," Richy chuckled.

Red didn't reply, and ignored Taite's entrance, busying himself instead pouring a shot from the whiskey bottle into his empty glass. "Another hand?"

Richy and Brent didn't answer, their attention was on the heated conversation between Taite and Sheriff Braddock at the saloon bar. Taite, a spare framed Irishman by descent, with a broken nose and a long brown coat that ran to his boots was prodding a finger violently in the space before Braddock's face.

"He's not for givin' up on them missing, steers," Brent said, then added. "An' who can blame him?"

The saloon owner, Isiah, had already made his way down to the arguing men. Standing on the other side of the bar, his hands resting on the polished wood, his white apron drawn up high under his arms. Isiah raised a hand and pointed towards the two men and then at the door to the saloon. It was pretty obvious he wanted them to take their difference of opinion outside.

Red stopped shuffling the cards and placed the deck down on the table. This was going to go one of two ways.

All around the saloon men had stopped drinking, eating, talking with their companions, all were watching the drama play out between Taite and the Sheriff.

Taite hesitated, then took a step towards the door. Braddock though, just hitched himself up higher on the tall chair and slung the remains of his whiskey down his neck before holding the empty glass towards Isiah.

Isiah didn't take the glass but said instead in a loud voice used to emptying saloon's, "Outside, now, sir."

Braddock's face reddened with temper, and he threw the glass toward the bartender. It bounced from his chest, rolled along the bar, hung for a moment on the edge of the wooden top, and with every eye in the saloon on it, fell to smash on the floor.

Red, sighing rose. "Excuse me gentleman."

Red approached the sheriff, a calm determination in his stride. When he spoke his words were quiet, not meant for the ears of the rest of those in the saloon. "Evening, Sheriff. I think you need to step outside."

Braddock turned on Red, his eyes bloodshot and defiant. The forefinger of his right hand prodding the badge pinned on his leather vest, he said, "You don't get to tell me what to do, Apache. I'm the law around here, and don't you damned well forget it."

Red felt a surge of anger but kept his voice steady. "It's time to leave. Every man in here thinks you are on Denver's payroll."

The sheriff sneered, reaching for his revolver, his hand resting on the top of the gun. "Now you just back off, son. We all know you were one of McKiddery's hired guns, and on the wrong side of the law."

Red shook his head slowly. "I'm not for makin' trouble, here, and neither is Isiah. It's time to leave."

The saloon was a study in silence. The occupants didn't move, all seeming trapped in time, only the dust motes in the shafts of the last rays of sunlight that came in over the saloon doors drifted in the air.

Isiah licked his lips, his eyes switching between both men, tiny beads of perspiration began to collect in the folds of fat on his brow.

The two card players were sat watching, like hounds in the chases, ready to move. No-one wanted to be the victim of a stray bullet.

"Don't," Red warned, the single word, was quietly spoken. A threat, a warning, but it was twisted by whiskey in Baddock's mind into a challenge.

Baddock's hand dropped to his gun.

Red was way quicker, his hand lightning fast as he drew his own gun, his reactions not slowed by liquor and age. "Don't make this a fight, Sheriff."

Braddock, fueled by whiskey and arrogance, fired first. Maybe it was meant as a warning, maybe it was just badly aimed, maybe he just mishandled the gun. He pulled the trigger before the gun was even out of the holster, the bullet ripped into the woodwork of the bar, tearing a long scar in the front beneath the polished top. The shot echoed through the saloon, and Red's own gun barked in response.

The bullet took Braddock full in the chest. He was still sat on the stool and for a moment he didn't move.

The men in the saloon looked between them, confusion on their faces.

Who'd been hit?

Then the sheriff's body crumpled, and he slumped on the seat. For a second it looked like he'd remain on the chair, then his body slowly keeled over sideways, his jaw slamming onto the top of the bar as he fell dead to the saloon floor. He landed on his side, and there for all to see was the gun, still in the holster.

Silence fell over the saloon as men stared in shock. Red holstered his gun. He hadn't wanted to kill the sheriff, but the damned fool had fired first.

Behind the bar, Isiah, pale faced, was shaking his head and looking between the dead man and Red in horror. "What you done, boy?"

# CHAPTER ONE

Oatman was a bustling mining town, silver and gold had lured men to her. The town's population seemed to have increased every time Nash arrived, as prospectors and miners flocked there, drawn by the promise of wealth.

On the outskirts the newly arrived set up their camps around the wagons they had brought until they staked their claims. Some would fail and end up working for other prospectors, long hours, backbreaking work and for what? There seemed to be only one man in Oatman who had struck it rich, and that was Mr. Vardy.

Vardy owned a dozen mines, controlled a gang of vicious men, one of the towns saloons and the two stores were also his. He profited from every aspect of life in Oatman.

The landscape around Oatman was rugged and desert-like, surrounded by mountains that were pockmarked with mines. Wooden structures, including saloons, general stores, and boarding houses, lined the dusty streets. And halfway along was where Mr. Vardy could be found, a single-story wooden building with a half dozen steps leading up from the street to a wooden veranda.

Mr. Vardy's office was the only solid structure near the mine. Thick wooden walls, small windows and a wooden roof. The door was always ajar, cigar smoke wafting from the inside, and two or three of Mr. Vardy's men would be propping up the walls outside, pieces on show, and eyes fixed unwaveringly on anyone near.

The wide hat brim shaded the face of the man approaching the office. Kip, Vardy's man, propped against the wall outside the office along with two other men, recognized him as Nash, and he straightened, thumbs tucking into his belt, the movement making the spurs on his boots rattle. Kip Jessop was a tall Mexican with a lean face, and a scar that twisted the right-hand side of his mouth into a permanent sneer.

When the man set his feet on the first of the three steps, he looked up over, the sun highlighting a face that had already been darkened by her rays. A close-cut beard covered his chin and square solid jaw. His face was marred by a scar, it split his right eyebrow in half then reappeared on his cheek, a knife wound, the blade had missed his eye but had sliced a line vertically down his cheek. An old wound, long since healed, but the scar stood out on the tanned skin.

Nash was shorter than Kip, of average height, he wore a faded and well-worn blue shirt, the fabric frayed at the cuffs and a little too tight at the shoulders, telling of the muscle below. His jeans held dust in the creases and were dotted with repairs, his boots though were well made, crafted from good leather, and there was polish beneath the days dust.

His eyes were blue, the color of sapphires, and the gaze they laid on Kip was unwavering. Across his hips was a gun belt, the piece in the holster on his right an old one shot and tucked into the belt to the left of this a curved hunting knife. On his back he carried a gun case, sewn out of leather, the carry strap running across his body.

Kip nodded his head towards a railing that ran around the front of the building and spat on the ground. "You know the rules, Nash."

Without a word, and with practiced ease, Nash released the buckle on the front of the gun belt. It slid from his hips, and he laid it over the top of the rail. It held an old Perry single shot breech-loader that had seen better days. The wooden grip was split and bound round with wire to keep it together. Kip regarded the weapon with a look of disgust.

Looping the strap over his head Nash took off the gun case he carried on his back and propped it against the rail next to his belt.

“What you got in there? A flintlock?” Kip scoffed.

“I do, she’s a good old hunting piece,” Nash replied, smiling weakly.

Nash didn’t say much, and today he’d said even less than usual. He’d ridden into Oatman two days ago with a dispatch for Mr. Vardy, and he’d been instructed to wait while Vardy penned a reply he wanted delivering to his partner in Bakersfield. It was a route Nash had covered many times and Vardy used him because he was reliable. What was in the letters Nash didn't care to know and that Mr. Vardy preferred to use a private route for his messages didn't bother him. Mr. Vardy paid and that was all that mattered.

But this time was going to turn out different.

Kip stared at Nash for a moment longer, he didn't speak, but instead twisted his head towards the door. Nash, used to the cold reception nodded again and made his way across the veranda, his boots stirring the dust on his way. Removing his hat, he stepped into the welcome of a smoky dark interior.

Mr. Vardy, as usual, was seated behind his desk. It always caught Nash's eye, the wood was topped with rich red leather, the edges patterned with gold. To the right was a set of scales, various weights sat next to them on a bent plate, and in the middle of the desk a wooden tray with small tightly tied bags, and beside them a smooth polished box with what looked like glittering shell set into the top which Nash knew contained money amongst other things.

"Nash," Vardy spoke around the side of the cigar, the smoke puffing sideways. Vardy's face wasn't clearly visible, his wide brimmed hat casting a shadow over his features, and they were further hidden behind the foggy veil of the smoke.

"Yes, sir," Nash replied, holding his hat respectfully against his chest, his head slightly bowed. Vardy was the boss, and he wanted everyone to know that. Nash, who had no interest in anything other than making a few dollars from working for him was happy to play the fool for Vardy. Happy to be seen as just another backwards trail cowboy who had a knack for making it across Indian territory. He was of no interest and no threat to Vardy, and that suited Nash just fine.

He just wanted a few dollars to take messages to Bakersfield and back. Simple work, it kept him on the plains, and he was a man who enjoyed his own company.

"I've more work for you, take this to my pard in Bakersfield, no wasting time along the way neither," Vardy's fat pale hand reached forward and lifted the fine ebony lid of the box, he withdrew a letter that he held towards Nash. It was much the same as many of the others he had taken to Bakersfield. A cream oblong of paper folded over with a seal on the back.

"You can rely on me, Mr. Vardy," Nash reached inside his jacket and pulled out a flat leather wallet, and taking the paper slipped it inside.

Vardy nodded, or at least seemed to, it was hard to tell. "You'll be paid by my pard, same as usual when you deliver."

"Yes sir, Mr. Vardy," Nash replied.

"One other thing. I've a man needs to get to Bakersfield, I'm in a hurry to get him there, and I've no mind to wait for a stage. I'd like you to take him," Mr. Vardy said.

Nash tried to find Vardy's eyes in the haze. "I like to travel alone, sir."

"Not this time, son. This time you got company and I'm counting on you to get him there," Vardy replied sternly, then raising a white hand he waved it towards the door, and called, "Kip, go find Ted."

"Thank you, Mr. Vardy," Nash said, nodding dutifully, he turned to leave.

"C'mon," Kip said as soon as he emerged.

Nash lifted the gun belt from where it lay over the rail. He buckled it back on, the metal fittings sliding back perfectly into their worn leather settings. He lifted the right side to get the fit right on his hips then slid his arm through the strap of the gun case.

The long-legged Mexican stalked off, but Nash easily matched his pace. Following him to where a tent was erected.

Kip stopped. "Murphy!"

A moment later the flap erupted, and a man emerged squinting into the daylight his hat in his right hand.

"This man'll get yer to Bakersfield," Kip announced, he bestowed a scowl upon them both before turning on his heel and returning to Mr. Vardy's office.

The man emerged fully from the tent, slid his hat onto his head, adjusted the brim and smiled towards Nash. "Howdy, sir."

"Murphy? From Ireland?" Nash asked hearing the man's accent.

"Yes, sir. Ted Murphy, born in County Down, miss it with all my soul. Irish through and through," Ted said smiling.

Nash looked Ted up and down. He was out of place, the dust of the plains hadn't yet eaten into his clothes and skin, he looked clean. Ted's hair, leaking from beneath his hat was overly long and the color of hot copper, you didn't see many like that, not out here on the frontier. Once Nash had a woman with the same copper red hair, or so he'd thought. Susie McGill had been her name, and when she'd taken the red burnished wig off and hung it on the bedpost before sliding out of her dress, he could still remember the acute disappointment.

"When do we leave?" Ted asked.

Nash let his eyes travel slowly over Ted again, and when they stopped, they met the man's eyes with a cold stare. "I'll take you, but that's it. I ain't feeding you, I ain't provisioning you, nothing else. I'll show you the trail, nothing more."

Ted grinned. "I'll be no trouble to you. None at all."

Nash doubted that very much.

# CHAPTER TWO

An hour later they left Oatman, heading east. Ted kicked his mare to bring her up next to Nash's and the two rode out in silence, Nash acknowledged Ted's presence next to him, but he had no mind to converse with the man.

Behind them, loping silently was a dog, his coat as rugged as the rocky terrain, the fur an unappealing mix of brown and grey, half of his left ear was missing, and what was left hung broken and floppy, and there was a slight limp to his gait in his hind quarters. Any quick glance in the hounds direction would see an old dog, advanced in years, worn and tired.

A frontier dog, hardened by cold and heat, worn by dust and wind. He'd pause occasionally, raise a grey scarred muzzle to the breeze and breathe in the scent of the landscape, then, seemingly satisfied his eyes sharp and alert he'd move with quick determination to catch up with Nash, falling in step again behind his horse. But if a man took the time and looked properly, and it was seldom that anyone did, they'd see the dog was young, battle scarred, wary and his eyes deeply intelligent and knowing.

Nash rode out easily on the trail, happy once again to be back in the saddle and heading away from the town. He'd been with the buckskin a good while; he treated her well and knew her ways. She was a proud horse with a golden coat that reminded him of a prairie sun, he kept her main long and untamed to match her spirit, it's color a dark brown, almost black, dancing in the wind. It matched her eyes, dark as bottomless pools, intelligent and holding the wisdom of the plains from eons past.

Called Nantai, Nash had named her for sunshine, all the light of the days sometimes seemed to be reflected in her coat. She remained only with him because she chose to, and Nash would have had it no other way. If there was no trust between man and beast then there could be no loyalty, and he'd not snare and hold an animal in slavery, it wasn't his way, or the way of those who'd raised him. She could keep up a solid pace for several hours without faltering, as long as he didn't push her too hard.

Nantai had the sturdy build and muscular frame of her breed, well-trained she exuded strength and endurance. Confident over rocky terrain, she could carry him for miles without faltering with a grace he had come to know and respect.

"Why's he keep doing that?" Ted asked breaking the silence, he'd swiveled round in his saddle, jerking a thumb in the direction of the dog.

"Doing what?" Nash said, not bothering to look towards his companion or the dog.

"Your dog. He keeps stopping and sniffs the air, what can he smell?" Ted asked, still looking back over his shoulder towards the hound.

"Plenty. But nothing that he wants me to know about," Nash replied, he was in no mood to talk.

"I don't know what you mean?" Ted said, then added. "Nothing he wants me to know about."

Nash just shook his head. "If he wanted me to know something he'd tell me."

After another short pause Ted, obviously keen to keep the conversation going, asked. "Does he have a name?"

"Rock," Nash replied bluntly before nudging the buckskin forwards and putting sufficient distance between him and Ted to end the conversation.

He liked the quiet of the plains and to have it broken by the alien Irish lilt grated on his nerves, the sound was wrong. Out of place. In a saloon perhaps, mixed with other Irish voices it would sound fine. But out here in the wilderness where the noise was from the wind, a gentle and soothing sound as it wound its way through the cacti and rocks, or the occasional rustle as a lizard scuttled beneath the undergrowth, the noise of distant thunder rolling across the plains, and the rhythmic sound from the hooves clinking on stone and shuffling the sand and pebbles of the desert. Ted's words pitched higher with his Irish ancestry and spoken quickly like a shake of a rattlers tail did not belong here.

They needed to go due west, skirting slightly south to avoid the worst of the Mojave, then angling back up again and heading west towards Bakersfield. To the north was Apache country and to the south Comanche, there was a thin no-man's land in between and this was where Nash was aiming for. He had always taken this trail alone, taking care as he rode. On one occasion he'd hidden in the rocks, the buckskin on her side next to him while the Commanche and Apache whooped and hollered and fought below him on the plains. When he'd emerged, at night, the fight was over, all that was left on the sands were dark patches where blood had leaked and two dead horses, once skewered through the eye and the other her throat cut – a mercy killing as white bone glinted in the moonlight where it had punctured the skin of one of her front legs. Nash had ridden through the night and then holed up again during the day. That was what it was like out here, and if there was trouble, he didn't like his chances of surviving it with the loud Irishman at his side.

Nash found the site he usually stopped at. It was next to a small trickling stream which would provide water for the horses, and there was enough buffalo grass sprouting near the bank to give the horses some grazing. In the distance to the north was a towering red rock cliff, set beneath a vast sky, as they unsaddled their horses the sky began to turn from the pale blues of the day to the warm yellows and deep oranges of sunset.

"Will you be looking at that! Never has a sun set so brightly since I was in Donegall,"

Ted said, his saddle held in front of him and coming to stand next to Nash.

Nash winced at the sound of the man's voice, and just nodded as he lifted his own saddle from the buckskin.

Nash set a small campfire inside a ring of rocks and brewed coffee while Ted, propped on his saddle watched. When the coffee was made, he set to sharpening his knife on a small whetstone he pulled from his pack. The dog was on the opposite side of the fire, lying next to Nash's saddle, the broken ear flopping down one side of his head and the other, erect and alert to the sounds of the evening.

"Rock, here boy," Ted called towards the dog.

Nash said reluctantly. "Don't go using his name, he'll not take to you."

Ted wagged his finger at Nash. "I've a way with dogs, sir."

"You might, I don't know you well enough to judge one way or the other. Rock, there, doesn't like white men," Nash paused in the act of sharpening his blade and used it to point towards the dog.

Ted, ignoring the advice, dug into his pack. He pulled out a parcel that contained jerky. Opening the packet, the spicey smell of pepper and smoky beef caught on the air, Rock's broken ear twitched and his eyes were rivetted on Ted.

"Smells, right good, don't it, boy," Ted said, peeling away two long dry aromatic strips. It was thick jerky, well-seasoned and made with care, it took a lot more drying and was trimmed of every scrap of fat to ensure it lasted well. It was expensive, the store in Oatman sold several types, and it seemed old man Scarrow had made a good sale when Ted walked through the door. It wasn't the jerky that Nash had stored in his pack, this was cheaper, no fancy herbs and pepper on it, just jerky, a little greaser than Ted's but that was the way he liked it. Taste, after all, didn't feed a man.

When he had time Nash made his own. It was good to know where it came from, how it was made. Thin strips cut with a sharp blade from a lean cut of meat, a flank or round, the fat trimmed away, a little salt rubbed into the meat was all he ever added, and then it was hung to dry. He doubted very much that Ted had ever stripped a joint of meat down to make trail food. If he had he'd have placed more value on the jerky, and in this wilderness, he'd not be offering it to a dog.

"Here, Rock, would you like this?" Ted was waving a long strip of dried meat towards the dog.

Rock fixed him with an unblinking stare.

"I've got his attention," Ted said triumphantly.

"Oh, I'd say that you have for sure," Nash said dryly, nodding.

Ted took his knife from the sheath and cut a goodly sized chunk from the end of the strip and stowed the knife away. "Here, Rock, do you want this?"

The dog just glared at him. It's feral eyes, from the other side of the fire unmoving.

"I'd say he's not that interested," Nash hoped he'd stop, this wasn't going to end well. Rock didn't like anyone. He'd warned Ted, it was fair that he had, and as far as Nash was concerned men only needed telling once. If he wanted to heed the warning then he would, if not then that was his choice. Telling and retelling someone was a woman's way. It made no difference, if a man had made a decision, then nagging him with the facts, as you saw them, wasn't going to change his mind.

Ted swung his arm back to throw the meat over the fire towards the dog. Before his arm had come forwards to complete the throw the dog had jumped. Rock cleared the fire, landing with his paws on Ted's chest and sending him backward to land sprawling on his back, the dog on top of him, the animals teeth sunk into his right wrist.

"Get him off," Ted howled.

Rock, his teeth working their way through the leather sleeve were twisting the arm, forcing his teeth further in towards the flesh. Ted screamed.

Cursing, Nash pushed himself up, caught the dog by the scruff of the neck, and pulled the dog off Ted. Rock unclamped his jaw, and growling menacingly released Ted. Nash pushed the dog roughly away, picked up the piece of jerky Ted had tried to throw and sent it to land next to his saddle. The dog circled the fire, picked the offering up, and swallowed it before resuming his position again next to Nash's saddle.

Ted was pushing his sleeve up. The dog's teeth had punctured the skin. Nash took hold of his wrist and examined it for a moment. "It's not bad."

"Is that it? your darn dog just tried to kill me," Ted said, his voice high-pitched with alarm.

"He bit your arm, it's not quite the same thing," Nash said, and added, "I told you he didn't like white folk."

"Your white?" Ted said.

"Well, yes, but I don't rightly know if he likes me either, I think he believes he owes me a debt," Nash pulled his pack towards him, and searching inside produced a small glass bottle stoppered with cork. "Show me your arm."

"What's that?" Ted asked, watching Nash pull the cork carefully from the top of the bottle.

"It's honey, and I don't know why, but it's mighty good for cuts," Nash said.

"It's not a cut, it's a bite," Ted said.

Nash fixed him with a hard stare. "You want me to fix you up or not?"

Ted relented and held the punctured wrist towards Nash. The liquid was clear and thick and ran from the bottle slowly onto Ted's wrist. "Rub it in and wrap it well to keep it clean."

Nash picked the cork stopper back up from where he had placed it carefully on a flat stone and pressed it firmly back into the bottle before storing it back inside his pack.

"Is that it? What do I wrap it with?" Ted said, his eyes switching between the pack and Nash.

Nash shrugged and pointed towards Ted's pack. "I don't know what you've got in there."

"Your dog bit me, it's the least you can do," Ted proffered the sticky injured wrist towards Nash.

"I told you, he doesn't like white folk," Nash said solidly, and turned his attention back to his own supper of jerky, his eyes back on the small fire again, watching the flames arc and dance inside the small ring of stones. Ignoring the cussing of the man next to him, as he rummaged noisily in his pack for something to wrap around his injured wrist. Ted finished and Nash heard the unmistakable sound of a cork popping from the glass neck of a bottle. Turning his head, he looked at the bottle Ted was tipping towards his lips.

"I wouldn't wash too much of that down your neck," Nash said.

Ted finished taking a long swig from the bottle. "Why? Will your damned dog attack me while I'm asleep?"

"Not the dog, but it's not good to lose your senses out here. Save it for when we get to a town," Nash said, he finished sharpening his knife, satisfied with the edge, he wrapped the whetstone back inside the leather pouch, tied the cord around it to secure it, and put it away inside his pack. He took out the makings and began to roll a cigarette, his eyes back on the fire, ignoring the noise of disorganization that came from Ted to his right. He could smell the whisky.

Out here it smelt bad.

It didn't belong, whisky was a smell that should mingle with tobacco smoke, men's sweat, the scent of drying leather and woodsmoke from a fire, and maybe even women's perfume. The smell of a saloon. It smelt bad when it was alongside the scent of the wilderness. Here the aromas were subtle, and yet distinctive, earthy and natural, tinted with the smell of the vegetation.

The smell of whisky continued to linger even though Ted had pushed the cork back in the bottle, the soft wood squealing in complaint against the glass as it was squeezed back in. The harsh pungent aroma of the liquor, like a predator, was chasing away the smell of the night, the dry earth, cacti and the smell of the pines they were camped near.

Ted had fixed up his wrist, and still grumbling, pushed his pack away, it was unfastened and tipped over, the whisky bottle rolling from it. Nash pretended not to notice.

"So, if Rock doesn't like white folk, who does he like? He looks like an Indian cur to me?" Ted observed, settling down with his back against his saddle again.

Nash didn't look towards Ted. "He was, and I suppose he still is, but he likes Indians even less than white folk. That's why he stops and sniffs the air, he's smelling for Indians."

"Does he like anyone?"

Nash shrugged. “Me, I guess.”

“So how come the cur hates everyone else?” Ted said, eyeing Rock.

“It’s a case of trust. He doesn’t like white folk, because he was trained not to trust them,” Nash said.

“How do you do that?” Ted asked.

“It’s easy. The Apache have white children in their camps, and they befriend the pups, give them a piece of meat then beat them with a branch. So, when you offered him a piece of that tasty jerky the next thing he expects from you is a beating. It was just a case of Rock getting in first, I guess,” Nash said, then waving an arm towards the dog he added, “And it works. The Apache know that the easiest way to get around a dog is the exact thing you tried, it’s easier than fighting it.”

“That’s how they train dogs?” Ted said, a little horrified.

“Yup, doesn’t take long, dogs learn fast,” Nash replied. “And if an Apache wants his dog to hate the Comanche, then he’ll do the same, get a Comanche prisoner to feed him and then beat him.”

“But you said he doesn’t like any Indians, not just Comanche?” Ted asked.

“Well, that’s because of how we met. He was with a raiding party of Apache bucks, and he got himself in the way of an arrow, went into his hind quarters, right to the bone, that’s why he walks with a limp,” Nash said.

“And you took the arrow out?” Ted asked.

"Eventually, he followed me for three days. Three days of him asking for help, and I thought if he's asking that hard then it ain't right for me to ignore him," Nash dropped the cigarette end and rubbed it out with his boot.

"Why did he follow you if he'd been trained to hate white folk?" Ted asked, "It doesn't make sense."

Nash smiled. "It does when Rock, there saw me kill the Apache who'd shot him. And I'm half Indian, maybe he was confused."

"Well, if he comes at me again, like that, I'd do the same," Ted said patting the holster at his side before pulling out the gun and turning it over in his hand. The metal shone, picking up the sunlight and reflecting it back.

"She's a beauty, don't you think?" Ted said, his eyes still admiring the piece.

Nash looked over. The holster was new, stiff leather, unscuffed, with no wear marks, and the colt was new. "Bet she set you back a fair few dollars."

Ted smiled. "It did, but she's sure worth it."

"You fired her much?" Nash asked.

"When I bought it in Oatman, there were targets set up. Tried two others, and this was by far the best shot. As you say, pricey, but like they said, a man can't afford to miss," Ted replied.

Nash nodded but kept his thoughts to himself. He knew the tactic, and he also knew the gun shop owner Old Man Tomlinson. Ted would have been given two other guns, the sights along the top of the barrel would be set askew putting off his aim, so when he took the new and expensive .44 in his hand and tried it, his shots would run true. They'd have congratulated him on his shooting skill and the deal would be done. Still, it was a nice piece, knowing what Ted wanted he held his hand out. "Let me feel the weight of her."

Ted, pleased, handed over his prized gun. "She's lighter than she looks, the grooves in the barrel there have got her weight down. And you can add a shoulder stock to her if you want."

"You bought that as well?" Nash asked, the gunsmith had gone to town on Ted it appeared.

"Yes, sir. It's in my pack," Ted reached over and pulled his pack closer, rummaging inside he pulled out a leather packet, releasing the cords to reveal a polished stock, the color of chestnut, smooth and perfect.

Nash reached over and took it, his fingers enjoying the cool perfection of the wood. "Colt sure makes good pieces. You know they call this revolver the McCulloch Colt?"

Ted shook his head. "I thought it was an army gun?"

"This here .44 was made from the big old dragoon, those weighed in around four pounds, which is a handful, I can tell you. It's got the power of the Navy but much smaller, and the weight is a little more, but not much," Nash hefted the gun in his hand, feeling the weight.

"Why did you call it the McCulloch Colt?" Ted asked.

"The war might be over, but another started up again, especially around Texas. With the troops all gone the fighting between the frontier types and the Indians started again. McCulloch persuaded Colt to make him an order of a thousand of these for the rangers, took some persuading as folks thought he was equipping his army again. But he did persuade them, and the rangers got these to fight against the Comanche and the like," Nash said, turning the gun over in his hand. "You can tell it's a military one, the back of the shield has been cut for the shoulder stock and there's this extra screw here."

Ted leaned forward to see where Nash was tapping his finger.

Nash pulled the rammer down. "And the manufacture marks are under here, hidden by the rammer. I like that."

"Why?"

Nash ran his hand down the smooth black barrel. "Gives it a clean look and a smooth feel."

"And she sounds good as well," Nash placed his thumb on the hammer and pressed it back. "Did you hear them? Four good solid clicks, a nice crisp action, strong spring with no slack in it."

Ted extended his hand, and Nash handed him the gun back. He pressed his thumb on the hammer and listened to the clicks.

"That's a Colt alright, even clicks, no give on the hammer, just nice and smooth," Nash said as he listened to the gun. "When the noise won't matter so much you can show me how she shoots."

Ted smiled, pleased. "I will, sir. What pieces are you carrying?"

Nash patted the Perry in his holster. "Just this old one shot and my rifle."

Ted, more interested in the rifle said. "What's the rifle, can I see it?"

Nash hesitated for a moment then leaned over and pulled the gun case closer. Ted watched as Nash unfastened the clips at the end of the leather holder that held his rifle.

"It's a Henry, isn't it?" Ted asked, pushing himself up on one elbow.

Nash just nodded and laid the gun down on top of the leather holder.

"I heard they can be unreliable," Ted said, "got a mind of their own and like to shoot a man's hand off when he's loading it."

Nash looked up. He had a rag in his hand and was polishing the brass on the gun. "Well, that's usually on account of the man, and not the gun."

"What do you mean?" Ted asked.

"When you load her, you slide this tab down here," Nash pushed a circular tab along the bottom of the gun barrel, "and this opens the tube at the top. Now you can slide in the rounds."

Ted raised himself to his knees to watch.

"Now a fool who drops a live round down the loading tube like this is likely to get his hand blown off," Nash held the gun vertical to show what he meant, "when you load her, keep the barrel just above level, let the rounds slide down nice and gently so they don't slam against each other, treat them with a bit of respect. When it's full they can't move so it's safe then to move her freely, there's a spring at the end there that keeps the rounds tight against one another."

"I've seen fools rest the stock on their foot and drop the rounds in. In my mind that's just asking for trouble, and that's why the Henry got a bad reputation sometimes. And another thing, if she's not full and you just let this tab here go it'll fire right back and slam into the rounds, you need to bring it down gently on top of them."

"Why wouldn't you fill her?" Ted asked.

Nash shrugged. "Maybe you don't have enough rounds left, or just not the time."

"Why don't you keep her loaded, then it's ready when you need it?" Ted asked, "If I had one, I'd want it ready should I need it?"

Nash turned over the barrel. "This is neat, there is a slot all the way down the back of the loading tube, and you can see the rounds you've put in."

Ted looked over and the long narrow slot revealed the line of bright brass cases that filled the tube.

"I can see when it's loaded, and how many rounds I got, but if you treat it bad and get dust and dirt in there then it'll jam. Not the gun's fault. That's why I keep her in a case. A man I used to know had one made with real soft lamb's wool on the inside, I was going to do the same until I saw it jam. There were twists of the wool caught between the rounds and they didn't slide down, you could see the tufts on the bottom of the barrel," Nash said. "So, I just got a plain old case made, and I make sure it's clean inside, and check the barrel every once in a while, to make sure she loads smoothly. And if I smell trouble, I keep her loaded," Nash handed the gun over to Ted so he could have a better look at it.

"Feels good," Ted said accepting the gun and holding it in both hands.

"I had the fortune to meet a man by the name of Benjamin Tyler Henry. He changed the gun the company were making, swapped the rounds, changed the lever action and it's named after him. It fires a .44 cartridge in a copper case, he made the lever action smoother than southern whiskey. Each gun has its own pressure, and you can feel the exact point the cartridge is going to drop into the gun," Nash said.

"Some say's the lever action makes it slow, but you don't think so?" Ted asked.

Nash shook his head. "When you've some practice in it's easy enough to hold her level and seek out a target while you slide another cartridge in. This was the first gun to give you a real second chance."

"What do you mean?"

"It's accurate, and if you've the misfortune to miss, and your aims a little off, then she'll let you have another try right away. I look after her, and she looks after me," Nash said, slowly and carefully he removed the cartridges, pressing each one back home into the leather loops in his gun belt. "I keep enough here to load her once."

"What you got on your hip?" Ted said, swiveling his head round to see the gun protruding from the holster on Nash's belt.

Nash smiled and patted the holster. "Nothing much, just a one-shot Perry. She's old but she's trusty, only a single shot gun, but she's served me well enough."

"Can I see her?" Ted asked.

Nash shrugged and pulled it from the holster handing it over. The grip was worn, split and bound with wire, dents and nicks in the grip darkened with wear and use. The barrel was scratched and it was in poor condition compared to the Henry Nash had shown him. Needing to say something, Ted said, "Feels well made."

Nash accepted the gun back. "She sure is."

What he didn't tell Ted was that sat in his pack were two .44 Colt's, loaded and ready to fire. Nash pulled his hat down over his eyes, settled down on the earth, and pulled a blanket around him. Ted was about to ask another question when he realized that the big man next to him was already asleep.

# CHAPTER THREE

The start of the second day was soured in more than one way. Waking up, Nash was welcomed with the smell of sour mash whisky. Ted hadn't righted the bottle and during the night the liquor had leaked around the badly fitting cork and dripped to the dry earth. Where there should have been the smell of morning, that subtle and yet delightful smell of the new day, there was just the overpowering aroma of the white man and his whisky. And Nash was fairly damn sure if he could smell it then so could others.

Rock, awake was still laid by Nash's saddle and watched as made coffee, it was a morning ritual he enjoyed. Boiling the water over a small fire, listing until it bubbled and popped in the small pot, then he'd tip in the aromatic coarse grounds and let the pot boil for another few minutes to allow the beans to release their flavor. Lifting the pot from the small fire Nash allowed it to brew, then to settle the grounds to the bottom of the pot he'd add a little more cold water, it was enough to send them to the bottom, so when he poured it carefully into his cup they remained in the pot. The cup in his hand, his blanket rolled up behind him and propped against a rock Nash settled back. The coffee had gone someways to overpowering the annoying smell of the whisky and when he got out the makings the smell of the tobacco wafting from the tin finished the job.

Ted was still asleep. He'd drunk too much whiskey, the fool. His hand wasn't that bad, a few small puncture wounds, he'd been lucky, his leather sleeve had saved him, and he was sure Rock was just giving him a warning. If the dog had been truly serious his white teeth would have found the soft flesh of Ted's face, Nash had seen the dog take a dislike to men before and it wasn't pretty. The dog was a killer alright.

Rock had risen himself when Nash made coffee. A hard life made him look older than he was. The limp and dented hind quarter where the arrow had been removed, the broken ear and the rough patchy coat were deceptive. Beneath the shaggy weathered fur rippled muscles, his eyes were sharp and alert and beneath the broken ear was a deep determination and intelligence that Nash recognized. He never underestimated Rock.

Ted stirred, uttered a grunt and emerged from beneath his rucked blanket.

"Howdy," Nash said.

Ted's eyes fixed themselves on the cup in Nash's hand. "That coffee smells mighty fine."

Nash dropped his eyes to his cup, he'd made one, and it was still over half full. Sighing he handed it to Ted; it might clear his thick head, and Nash could do without having a man not fully in possession of his senses on the trail today.

Ted tipped his head back and drank from the cup, then to add further insult he wiped his hand across his mouth and discarded the last of the coffee onto the dry earth. Seeing Nash's raised eyebrows he said, "It was getting a might gritty towards the bottom."

"It's how you drank it that's the cause of that," Nash replied taking his cup back from Ted. Drying it carefully, he put the pack of coffee grounds back inside it and stowed it in the middle of his pack. Rock was back, and Ted eyed the dog nervously.

"Just ignore him, and you'll be fine," Nash reassured.

"Have no fear of that," Ted said, "Look his furs covered in blood!"

Nash cast a quick glance towards Rock, the fur around the dog's mouth was bright red. "I guess he had a cotton rat or such like for breakfast."

Ted watched him clear the camp but made no move to help. Instead, he just kept up a tiring, and unwanted barrage of questions. Nash was looking forward to saddling up and getting back on his horse, they'd rode in comparative silence the day before, and he was hoping this would be the same today.

"Why are you brushing those stones down, seems a strange thing to do?" Ted asked, his hand slapping on his neck where an insect had bitten him.

Nash's shoulders dropped. He picked up another stone from his right that had not been near the fire and offered it to Ted.

"Here, smell it?"

"What do I want to smell a rock for?" Ted said, recoiling from the dusty stone.

"Just take it," Nash proffered it toward him.

Ted, rolling his eyes took the rock and sniffed it before dropping it.

"And what can you smell?" Nash said patiently.

Ted looked both confused and annoyed at the same time. "Nothing, it's a rock."

Nash offered him one that had surrounded the fire. "Now this one."

Ted took it. "It smells of the smoke from the fire."

"Exactly," Nash said, taking the stone back from Ted. "And you might not be able to smell that unless it's right in front of your nose, but you can bet an Apache can, and if he misses it his dog will sure let him know."

Ted accepted this and continued to watch Nash. He buried the ashes from the fire, smoothing clean earth over the top, sealing them beneath. He'd already dusted the rocks and then pressed the scorched sides into the ground, and taking a handful of sagebrush he'd gathered, he rubbed the leaves roughly in his hands releasing the juice from them and then rubbed that over the tops of the rocks. "Sagebrush is mighty pungent and disguises the smell of the fire. I've already made sure it doesn't look like there's been one and now, hopefully, it won't smell like there's been one either."

Nash took up some earth and dusted his hands with it, drying them of the plants juice. Rising, he began to leave the camp.

"Are we leaving?" Ted asked, beginning to rise, his hand going to his neck again. "I swear I am being eaten alive!"

Nash smiled. "Well, I guess while they are eating you, they are leaving me alone."

"Isn't that the truth," Ted said, irritation in his voice.

Nash picked up the crushed sagebrush and turned it in his hands. "It's a mighty fine plant, might not look it, but it sure is. You take this and rub it between your hands and then rub your neck. Those critters don't like the smell, and they'll likely leave you alone."

Ted accepted the twigs and crushed leaves doubtfully. "Are you sure?"

Nash smiled. "Just ask yourself which of us is scratching like a dog full of fleas."

"I guess so," Ted began to rub the sagebrush between his hands releasing more of the earthy scent.

"If you run short on coffee it makes a passable drink. You just hunker down there, Rock and me'll be back soon. It doesn't go well to set off on the trail before you know who else is on it," Nash explained before settling his hat on his head and turning to leave the camp, Rock trailing behind him.

# CHAPTER FOUR

Nash, heading towards where they had left the horses hobbled grazing near the stream stopped in his tracks when he heard Rock growl behind him. Whatever it was the dog had sensed was down near where the horses were. To Nash's left was a rock and he crouched down behind it, flipping the loop on his holster he had the Perry in his hand, his eyes fixed on the vegetation ahead.

"Go on," he said quietly to the dog. And Rock took off through the sparse undergrowth behind to Nash's left, skirting round behind the horses. Nash watched and listened, whatever scent or noise Rock had detected was too far away for him to hear, and the slight breeze travelling up the slope from where the horses were carried nothing with it.

Nash waited. Patience in itself was a key to survival. He'd wait until Rock came back or he heard from the dog.

Ted, tired of waiting, and audibly grumbling tramped down from the top of the slope carrying his saddle. Nash twisted round; he was about to warn Ted when a shot rang out. Ted was no longer standing, Nash swung round forwards, the shot had come from where the horses were. From behind him he could hear the noise of Ted; the shot had knocked him from his feet. Staying low, Nash made his way between the sparse brush to where Ted lay, on his back, his saddle covering his chest and blood trickling from his temple.

"Are you hit?" Nash said, pulling away the saddle.

"No ... yes .... I don't know," Ted stammered, his face pale.

There was no telltale plume of blood spreading through his clothing. The bullet had punched a hole into the seat of the saddle and ripped the back of the cantle apart where it had exited. Reaching down Nash pushed Ted's hair away from the blood. "You cut your head on the rocks when you fell, your saddle took the bullet. Stay down."

Ted, unarmed, was of little use to him.

Returning to the cover of the bolder, Nash looked down below him. This time he did see something. A man was moving slowly from the cover of the trees. He must have seen Ted go down and was making his way up the slope towards where he had fallen. It was a gait Nash recognized immediately even though his face was hidden by his hat.

Kip.

He also saw something else. Behind Kip, low to the ground, moving silently, his eyes fastened on his target was Rock. The dog was stalking him, and Nash knew what he would do, moving quicker than Kip when he got close enough, he'd rise from the ground propel himself forward and land on the man's back, his teeth sinking into his neck. Nash waited, the closer Kip got the better shot he'd have, and Rock seemed to appreciate this as well and made no move to attack.

It was too late.

Kip was halfway towards Ted now, and he could see from the expression on the Mexican's face that he'd seen where he was, and worse, that his quarry was not dead.

"Leave him be, Kip," Nash said standing slowly, his gun pointing towards the Mexican.

The sun hung low in the sky, casting long shadows over the endless plains. Dust swirled in the dry air, and the distant sound of a rattlesnake echoed ominously. Nash stood his ground, boots planted firmly in the parched earth, his eyes narrowed against the glare. Across from him, Kip, with a reputation for a bad temper as fierce as the desert sun, smirked, in his hand his revolver, pointed now towards Nash.

"Does that piece you're actually holding even fire? Think you could take me, Nash?" Kip laughed, his voice dripping with arrogance. His dark eyes gleamed with a dangerous light, reflecting the fire of a man who had danced with death more times than he could count.

Nash remained silent.

"It's not your fight, why don't you push on out of here. You got one chance," Kip said, an evil smile flickering across his lips.

Nash shook his head. "I don't' think I'll take it," then to Ted. "Ted, you get yourself back up that hill and out of sight, do you hear me?"

A shuffling of feet told that Ted had heard him clearly enough.

"He's a good fur nothin' cur, why are you helping him?" Kip complained.

"Mr. Vardy told me to take him to Bakersfield, and that's what I'm going to do," Nash replied.

"I got news for you, things have changed," Kip said, then shrugged. "No matter, if it's one or both of you."

In that split second, the world erupted into chaos.

Gunfire rang out, the sharp cracks echoing against the backdrop of the vast landscape. Dust exploded around Nash, mingling with the sound of bullets whizzing past. Nash ducked low, using the sparse brush for cover. He rolled to his left, tucked himself behind a bolder. He could almost feel the heat from Kip's shots, each one a reminder of how high the stakes had become. But Nash wasn't about to back down. He had one shot, and he'd use it well. He steadied his breath, focusing on the rhythm of his heartbeat. With a quick glance, he spotted Kip's silhouette against the sun—a shadow of menace. Nash tightened his grip on his gun, his resolve hardening.

With a sharp exhale, he rose from his cover and fired with practiced ease. One shot only in contrast to the Mexican's barrage of random fire. The bullet flew straight and true, finding its mark. Kip staggered back; shock written across his face as he clutched his side. The outlaw's bravado evaporated, replaced by the harsh reality of the moment.

Nash approached cautiously.

Kip was now on his knees, the fight fading from his eyes.

"You should've known better than to mess with me, Kip," Nash said, his voice steady but filled with the weight of what he'd done.

"I... I didn't think you had it in you," Kip gasped, his defiance crumbling.

"Why'd you want to shoot Ted?" Nash said, leaning down over the dying man.

Kip didn't reply. He swayed for a moment before he pitched forwards and fell on his side in the dust, his piece a foot away from where it had fallen from his hand, his hat was still in place. Nash placed his boot on the man's shoulder and forced the body to roll onto its back. As it turned over the hat caught the breeze, hovering for a moment over Kip's head then it wheeled away bouncing between the sagebrush.

Nash just stared into the lifeless eyes. The man's last breath still lingered around them, his soul still caught for a moment between life and death. The expression on the face of shocked surprise would, Nash knew, melt soon enough. The creases around the eyes and mouth would relax, and the eyes, rather than holding the Kip's final moment would soften to a blank death stare. Apache called it nuishi. Dead, and yet not gone, that moment before the soul, the nui, left on its eternal journey.

It was rare to see.

Nash could hear Ted behind him, his boots scrabbling over the rocks. "You got him?"

Nash didn't reply. All souls, good or bad, deserved respect. There was nothing the dead man could do now to harm him. Nash had taken from him the gift of life, they were, if anything, even.

Ted was getting closer.

Kip's eyes had dimmed, and were no longer as wide, the mouth with the lips curled back revealing blackened teeth had relaxed, the lips not closed, but they had drawn back together.

Kips nui was gone.

Ted had clearly seen the body sprawled before Nash and a moment later he was at his side.

"All the saints! It's Kip!" Ted gasped arriving in a flurry of dust and grit, his hand had found Nash's upper arm and was clamped around it, the nails biting through his shirt. Nash roughly shook off the hold.

"It's Kip, alright," replied Nash. He crossed to where Kip's piece lay in the dirt and retrieved it. The revolver was worn, a testament to countless dusty trails and showdowns. Its barrel, slightly tarnished and scratched, reflecting a history of use, with hints of rust creeping along the edges where the metal had been exposed to the elements. The once-bright bluing had faded to a dull grey, giving it a rugged, seasoned appearance. The grip, crafted from polished wood, bore the marks of time and careless use, nicks and dents dark marks in the wood. The barrel was scratched. Nash spun the chamber – he'd counted right – the gun was empty.

Leaning down Nash took hold of the leather tongue of the gun belt and hauled it back to release the pin from the buckle, then he pulled it free of the dead man.

"Why'd he try to shoot us?" Ted asked as he watched.

"Here, hold this," Nash handed the gun belt to Ted and returned to Kip, leaning down he began to check his pockets.

"What are you doing?" Ted said aghast, the gun belt hanging limply in his hand.

"I sure as Hell ain't leaving a gun and bullets here that someone could pick up and turn on us," Nash said, he'd finished and began to push lose bullets he'd found into the loops on Kip's belt.

"Come on, we're leaving," Nash said striding back towards their camp.

"Why?" Ted said, hard on his heels.

"I'd like an answer to that question as well?" Nash said, not breaking his stride on the way back to the camp.

"What's the rush? He's dead!" Ted was running to catch up.

Nash stopped abruptly. "I don't know why he came after us, maybe you do. But his horse has fled, and we got maybe three hours before they know in Oatman that's Kip's missing. So, we leave."

Nash moved down to where the horses were. They were still hobbled but agitated by the shots that had shattered the peace of the morning. They saddled in haste and strapped their packs back on. Nash took the Henry from its case and took fifteen cartridges sliding them in carefully. He secured the gun to the left side of his saddle and the pair left their camp. While they made their rapid preparations to leave they heard the sound of Rock growling, the dog was not treating his victim as deceased and with lips curled back was viciously tearing at Kip's face, flaps of flesh hung from the dead man's skull.

"You gonna let him do that?" Ted asked nervously.

Nash shrugged. "Ain't my dog. Doubt if he'd stop anyway."

"It's not ...."

"It's not what?" Nash asked.

"It's not Christian," Ted said, his eyes being drawn to the scene of the dog and the mangled corpse.

"Well, that's alright, cos Rock ain't a Christian either," Nash said coldly.

# CHAPTER FIVE

It was several hours before Nash slowed the pace, and he brought his buckskin next to Ted's.

"So why has Mr. Vardy sent Kip after you?" Nash asked.

"Me?" Ted gawped at him; his voice high pitched.

"Well I been working for him for a year and he's not had incident to take against me, so I'm guessing it's you," Nash replied, he pulled his horse to a stop.

"Mr. Vardy has no reason to take against me, I'm working with him?" Ted protested.

Nash, shaking his head, pulled the leather packet from inside his waistcoat that held the letter he'd been given by Vardy to deliver. He waved the packet towards Ted. "I go back an' forth to Bakersfield delivering these. It used to pay well."

"What do you mean it used to?" Ted said.

"Kip's Vardy's man, if he's out here shooting at us then I think it's fair to say I'm not working for him anymore," Nash contemplated the leather pouch for a moment longer, then untying it he drew out the white sealed letter.

"You can't open that?" Ted blurted.

Nash fixed him with a cold stare. "Have you forgotten already what just happened?"

"It can't be Mr. Vardy, there's got to be some other explanation," Ted continued to object.

Nash's thumb broke the seal on the letter, and he unfolded the page and stared at the sheet.

"What is it?" Ted said. Then when he still didn't receive a reply. "Let me see."

Nash held the sheet towards Ted who took it.

"I don't understand," Ted said, confusion on his face as he raised his eyes from the paper to meet Nash's gaze.

"You don't understand much today, do you?" Nash said. "Vardy wants rid of you. He's sent you out of Oatman with me. Kip most likely left before we did. He knows where I camp on my first night, that's why Rock didn't pick him up following us. He's sent me to Bakersfield, but he knew I'd not be arriving, that's why he gave me that blank page. He just wanted you out of Oatman before you disappeared. So why were you going to Bakersfield?"

"To register a claim with his partner," Ted said weakly.

A frown creased Nash's brow. "You don't need to go to Bakersfield to do that, you can do it at the mine office in Oatman?"

Ted shook his head. "It's a big strike. To make sure it was fully legal ...." Ted's words trailed off and his face paled. "Oh, my dear Lord and all the saints! That means ...."

"Exactly," Nash agreed grimly. "I'd lay a wager that a claim has already been staked at the mine office on that land you hoped to work."

Ted's hold on the reins had slackened, his eyes unfocused staring ahead of him.

"No point dwelling on it now. We've another problem we gotta deal with," Nash said.

"What's that?" Ted asked, his voice a little distant.

"We got Comanche to the south, and Apache to the north. And I don't want to use the trail I normally take in case Vardy sends someone else after us," Nash explained.

"So where do we go?" Ted asked.

"Well, we sure as hell ain't going back to Oatman, or on to Bakersfield. So, we cross to the north, and then arc down south of Bakersfield," Nash said, an arm pointing ahead of him in the direction he intended to take.

They rode on in silence for the rest of the day, and when the sun was dipping towards the horizon Nash found a place to camp and called a halt.

“Not wise to light a fire tonight,” Nash said as he pulled his blanket from his pack. “We’ll get a few hours’ sleep and leave early.”

Being shot at seemed to have curbed Ted’s tongue, he was quiet that evening, although Nash did notice that night before he wrapped himself in his blanket, he finished the whiskey that was left in the bottle.

The following day Ted seemed in a better mood. “I been thinking, there’s got to be a way I can get my claim back.”

Nash shrugged. "Might be, I don't know."

"Vardy can't just cheat me out of it and take it for himself. It's a valuable claim, maybe a lawyer will help me for a cut of it's worth," Ted ventured.

Nash looked over a Ted, but didn't reply.

"What do you think? Maybe if I go to a big city, I'll find someone who'll help. That's what I'm thinking I'll do," Ted continued.

"Could work. I don't know much about the law," Nash said. What he did know was that it mattered very little what any fancy man in an office in city said or wrote, none of that held any sway with men like Vardy. The only law was their law, and it was enforced by men like Kip. "Vardy's men are mean, Hector Wainright, the Sheriff's one of them, so there's not much point in complaining in Oatman. The Vardy boys, as they call 'em, do as they please."

"You sure?" Ted said uncertainly.

Nash shook his head and pointed behind them. "What evidence do you need. He sent one of his boys after you. Vardy has a big house on the edge of town and his men live in the ranch house close by. If they want anything they just take it."

"Really, you sure about the Sheriff, I met him ..." Ted said.

"Yeah, I'm damned sure. I just got back to Oatman, and I heard what happened to Madge Fuller, did that pass you by?" Nash said roughly.

Ted shook his head. "A week or so back, while I was on the trail, the Vardy boys left Dante's saloon, skins full of whiskey, and seen Madge Fully, daughter of one of the miners. They'd taken the poor girl back to their ranch house. She'd screamed for help when she'd been pinned over the front of Kip's saddle, but no one had dared to stop them. She was found dead the following morning at the bottom of Byers Gill."

"I heard some poor woman had had an accident," Ted said shaking his head.

"Accident!" Nash scoffed. "The Sherrif, Wainright, declared that all the girl's injuries were due to the fall. Whether she'd jumped or been pushed no one would ever know," Nash waved a finger in front of Ted's face. "She'd been raped so bad her innards had come out. Doc Jerrod saw the poor girl. He's sure she choked to death."

"Choked?"

"Yeah, and I'll let you figure out what on. Those are the men you're dealin' with. Mr Vardy's good ol' boys."

The color drained from Ted's face.

"And that's not the only time, neither. Usually the women don't turn up," Nash said.

"But you work for Vardy?" Ted said.

"I deliver his messages. That's all. He thinks I'm a half-wit who can cross Indian country with his messages, and right now it suits me to take his money," Nash replied roughly.

They rode on in silence after that. Nash wasn't going to voice his opinion, Ted had just lost his claim, probably all he owned, and someone had tried to take his life as well. The man just didn't need more bad news to heap on top of all that.

"I can smell a cooking fire?" Ted said, pulling his horse alongside. "Are there any homesteads on the trail? I'm getting mighty hungry."

Nash had noticed the smell quite a while back, and Rock before that. His broken ear was turned forwards, listening, and he'd stop regularly and raise his grey and brown muzzle to the air. Nash liked the way dogs did that. One thing at a time and do it well. A dog smelling the air, would stand stock still, often they even closed their eyes, the only sense that mattered was smell. Drawing in air, pulsing it through their nostrils.

It wasn't a good smell.

And despite what Ted thought it certainly wasn't a cooking fire.

Ahead was a ridge, the land rising gently towards it, there was little vegetation, just low scrub amongst the scattered rocks, nowhere for anything to hide. The smell of smoke was stronger now. Rock stopped again, and this time so did Nash. Ted just carried on, the sound of the hooves on the dusty earth seeming louder than they should have. Small clouds of yellow-grey dust rising from around the prints left by the metal shoes.

Rock growled.

A low grumble, deep from within his chest. The sound was a warning for Nash, it was a noise that wasn't meant to carry.

Ted reached the ridge, the first to be able to see what lay below. Nash rode up next to him.

Twenty feet below them was a fire, the flames now out, but it was still smoldering and sending smoke up the ridge towards them. Across the fire lay a body.

As they descended the ridge and got closer Nash could see that the fire had taken hold of the body. Catching first on dry cloth, then travelling to the leather belt and shirt where it fed faster, the flames hotter, and soon it turned its voracious appetite on the man's flesh. The skull was burnt to the bone, the skin blackened and crisped, the mouth open, lips dried by fire had receded bestowing a humorless leer on the new arrivals. The top of his skull was visible, the zigzagged passage of the bone where the halves were fused a dark line in the grey burnt bone.

The body was only partly consumed by the fire. His right arm, outstretched, was unburnt from the elbow down over. The cuff of a once blue dusty denim shirt still encircled his wrist, the fire seemed to have stopped there. The hand, white, pasty, inanimate, still clawed in the dust where he'd fallen. Before it was the flattened patches where moccasins had left their impressions and splats of dried blood scattered around them. It was a grim scene; they'd taken his scalp before they'd left him to burn.

Behind the corpse the dust was rucked and twisted with confusion. Nash held his hand up. "Stay there."

Ted, pale, his eyes fixed on the burnt man shifted uneasily on his horse.

Nash circled the clearing. There'd been a wagon there, just the one. It had come in from the west, then it had been turned and headed south. Hoof prints and a pile of drying horse shit that was entertaining the flies the only evidence it had been there. Tracks, thin lines in the dirt, told where the wagon had been driven off.

Whoever he was had lost not only his life but his possessions to the Indians.

"We're leaving," Nash announced suddenly, he didn't need to see more, the wagon had gone south, some hours ago, and that meant they would avoid that route, turn west along the ridge and follow it a way before changing direction.

Rock was busy.

His teeth engaged and swinging his head from side to side in that way dogs do when trying to shake the life from some animal or tear something apart, in this case it was the latter.

"You gotta stop him," Ted pointed towards the dog, his face pale.

Nash shrugged. "Why?"

It took a while, but the dog got what he wanted in the end, pulling the burnt arm away at the elbow Rock disappeared towards a large patch of sagebrush, and some shade, with his prize.

"Shouldn't we do something?" Ted said again, his voice high pitched.

Nash leaned forward in his saddle. "You're thinking we should bury him, right?"

Ted shook his head. "Seems the Christian thing to do."

"I'm sure it is and I'm sure he'd appreciate your sentiment. And if you want to, I'll not stop you. But I'd like to point out the ground is harder than nails, sure there's dust at the top, but once you get a few inches down it's like digging through iron. You've no shovel, so I suppose you'll be digging with your hands, that'll be mighty hard and sore work for you. Or you could cover him with rocks, that'll keep the birds off for a while, or at least until some coyote gets a scent of what's beneath them and digs their way in. So, you can if you want, do the Christian thing, but I'd suggest if your conscience is botherin' you that much you might just want to say a few words instead."

Ted cast his eyes around the clearing.

Nash gave voice to Ted's thoughts. "There's not enough rocks to do the job either, you'll be hefting them from some distance, an' in this sun …."

Rock growled. A low menacing sound. Nash turned in his saddle. Behind him the dog was stalking towards a thicket of sagebrush, his meal forgotten, lips curled away to reveal sharp white canines, the hairs along his spine bristling.

Nash waved Ted back, in a second the Henry was in his hands. He nudged the mare forwards, so she was behind Rock. Whatever the dog had sensed was hidden in the thicket. Rock's growl intensified. Almost within reach of the bush he lowered his head, his eyes fixed upon something and released a vicious snarling bark before darting forwards.

"Call him off or I'll shoot!" The voice was high pitched, filled with fear and female.

"Rock, back!" The command from Nash was enough, he'd done his job and retreated, emitting now only a threatening low growl. "You can come out, ma'am, he'll not hurt you."

The brush moved, the twigs bending and snapping, and from them emerged a woman. She was wearing a green dark check men's shirt and long dark grey pants, perfect camouflage, the brush had snagged in her hair, scraped her face and torn into the sleeves of her shirt. Nash was guessing she'd thrown herself into the bush in a hurry, and who could blame her, a few scrapes and cuts was a preferable fate to what had happened to the man in the fire.

"Ma'am, they've gone. I'm Nash, this here is Ted, and we were on the trail when we saw the smoke," Nash said, his voice calm, as yet he'd not slid his gun back into its holder or descended from the saddle.

The woman forced her way from the thicket, stumbling, and pulling her shirt sleeves free with her left hand, her right hand, trembling, weighed down by the gun. The Colt looking huge in her small hand. Almost free from the snare of bristle and twigs she took one more step forward and her foot caught under a root, she emitted a cry, and fell forwards, her right hand instinctively tightened on the gun, the trigger depressed and the shot rang out, the ground erupting before her in a plume of yellow grey dust. A moment later the woman, unable to save herself, landed face down in the rising dust.

Nash secured the Henry back in the holder and dropped from his saddle. In three quick paces he made it to the fallen woman, and kneeling, unfurled the woman's fingers from the gun, saying, "Just in case, ma'am."

Ted, his hands over his ears arrived, a flurry of agitation. "Ma'am, you need to have a care with that."

Nash, the gun tucked into his own belt, and with a hand under the woman's arm was lifting her up. When she looked at him it was from eyes rimmed red with crying, her face dust streaked. She wiped the back of her hand across her face, and sniffing, attempted to regain her composure. "That's mighty kind, sir, I don't know what I'd have done if you'd not stopped."

"That shot will have been heard for some distance. How long is it since those Indians left here ma'am?" Nash asked.

"A few hours ... maybe," the woman replied hesitantly.

"I'm afraid we need to leave, if you've a mind, you can ride behind me," Nash said, his hand still on her arm. She said nothing, but just nodded.

With a practiced ease, Nash fitted his boot into the stirrup and rose back into his saddle. Moving the mare to the left, he leaned down and extended an arm towards the woman. She hesitated for a moment only, before she took it, and he pulled her up to ride behind him.

Ted, confused, cast his eyes around. “We’re leaving?”

“We are. Everyone for a dozen miles heard that shot,” Nash had already turned his horse away from the other man and was leading her from the clearing. He had a mind to put a good many miles between themselves and the grisly discovery they had made as quickly as possible. He sent his mare into a gentle jog, and when sure that the woman behind him was holding on well he increased the pace.

# CHAPTER SIX

Nantai was carrying two, not that the woman behind him was overly heavy, the two saddle bags he had probably weighed neigh on the same. And she was good to his horse. Shifting her position behind him only when she needed to, not holding on too tightly, keeping her feet still and away from Nantai's sides.

The horse trotted steadily along the dusty trail, her powerful legs moving rhythmically in a smooth, flowing motion, Nash holding the reins with a firm yet gentle grip. As the horse's hooves struck the ground, a soft thudding sound echoed in the quiet of the open landscape. The trail wound through sagebrush and wildflowers, Nash's eyes scanning the horizon for any danger ahead of them.

The rhythmic motion of the trot created a sense of calm, and he could feel the woman behind him relax and unwind, the tension leaving her body as the journey progressed and they put more distance between her and the horror behind them.

The woman didn't speak at all on that first journey, and Nash was thankful for that, giving his full concentration to where his mare's shod feet were going, on the terrain ahead, and on that around them.

When he pulled Nantai to a slowing halt the light was starting to dim in the skies. They'd come a long way, Ted, on his right had been complaining about the pace, but had finally shut up when he realized Nash wasn't going to reply.

Where he'd chosen to stop wasn't ideal, but it was the best place he'd seen and if he waited much longer, they would be trapped by the darkness. They stopped at the top of a small narrow ridge, it gave an all-round view of the land, and to the east it sloped down towards a stream where there was shelter and grazing for the horses, and they would be more or less out of sight. From the ridge they could keep a watch and see if they had been followed. Nash looked at his two travelling companions – it was going to be a long night.

Turning in his saddle he extended an arm towards the woman, and she took it, lowering herself to the ground. She was stiff, and he wasn't surprised. It had been a long ride without a saddle, but she'd borne it without complaint, which was more than could be said for Ted.

"Keep your eyes on the horizon over there," Nash said to Ted pointing.

Nash took a wrapped leather roll from his pack and released the leather ties. Lined with soft sheepskin on the inside it opened to reveal a foot of shining brass, the metal wasn't perfect, and the dents reflected the dying sun's light in different ways giving the tube a jeweled look.

"Is that one of them spyglasses," Ted asked, intrigued and leaning forwards.

Nash didn't reply, he raised it to his eye and scanned the horizon slowly.

"Can you see anything?" Ted said.

"Still your words. It takes time. Those braves are like lizards, they blend in with the land. You have to look real closely. They'll not make it easy for you," Nash replied, still scanning the land around them.

Ted, with the impatience of a child huffed and continued to watch Nash. When Nash finally lowered the glass, he said. "Well, anything?"

"Can't say as there ain't and can't say that there is," Nash replied.

"Well, that's darn helpful," Ted said, annoyed.

"Just because I can't see them doesn't mean they aren't there," Nash said.

"What's the point in having that then?" Ted pointed towards the spyglass.

"Because I might have seen them," Nash said beginning to secure the telescope back in its sheepskin roll.

"Can I look?" Ted said eagerly.

Nash looked between the telescope and Ted and sighed. "Here, be careful."

Ted accepted it grinning. "It's heavier than it looks."

"So don't drop it," Nash said reluctantly releasing his hold on the telescope.

"My Uncle has one. Longer than this, mind you. He's in the navy," Ted said, standing and scanning the horizon.

"Does he," Nash said, watching Ted as he turned and surveyed the land around them.

"Even looking through this there's nothing to see out there," Ted said, lowering the telescope.

"Looking and seeing ain't quite the same thing," said Nash accepting the scope back and wrapped it back in the wool lined case. "I'll take the horses down there for water. I'll leave my Henry up here, just in case you need it."

"Bring some back up for me as well," Ted said taking the last drink from his canteen.

"Ma'am, would you care to help me?" Nash asked, a kind note in his voice.

She nodded and took the offered reins of Ted's horse from him.

"Ma'am, I'm sorry you've had such a tough ride today," Nash said, apologetically.

She looked at him strangely. "I think I should apologize, sir, that was a foolish thing I did, pulling the trigger like that. I should have known better."

"Well, ma'am, it wasn't ideal, but not something you could help," Nash replied.

"Thank you for saying so, sir. But I do know when I've done a foolish thing, and as my pappy used to say, sometimes honesty is all we got left," she replied, "and right now I don't have a lot else."

"What happened?" Nash asked.

"I was travelling with my Uncle Clem, the Indian's burnt us out of our homestead, set fire to the roof at night. The smoke got to my aunt's lungs, and she died a few days back, and Uncle Clem was taking me to his brother's house near Goldsprings," She replied quietly.

"I'm sorry to hear that, ma'am. There's a lot of trouble at the moment," Nash said.

"Sure is. We traded with the Indians, Uncle Clem sold them horses, Aunt Milly made these delicate little crochet patterns that they liked to buy, I thought we were friends," she said shaking her head.

"I think they felt the same. There's been a lot of lying, and it's folks like you that's suffered for it, I reckon," Nash said, his voice serious.

The woman stopped, switched the reins from her right hand to her left, and held it out towards him. "I'm Lucy, sir, and I have yet to thank you for your timely arrival."

He took her hand briefly in his and let it go immediately. "Some might say we arrived a little late, ma'am."

"There wasn't a lot you could have done, there were a dozen of them, Uncle Clem saw them coming, threw his gun at me and told me to run. They didn't see me, and after they'd killed him, they didn't stay long. Two of them took Uncle Clem's wagon, and left whooping and a' hollering. Leaving the poor man to burn in his campfire where he'd fallen," the bottoms of her eyelids were wet, and she blinked away the tears quickly.

"I'm sorry ma'am," Nash said, a little awkwardly.

She took in a long breath, straightened her back and stepped forwards again with the horse. "It was quick, and Aunt

Milly didn't have to see it which was a blessing from the Lord."

"I'm sure it was, ma'am," Nash said, feeling he had to say something in reply.

Lucy sniffed loudly and rubbed her nose. "Sir, I'm sure Aunt Milly and Uncle Clem would be thanking you as well if they could."

"Thank you, ma'am," Nash stepped forwards, the buckskin, her nostrils scenting water, obediently followed.

At the bottom of the incline a narrow stream ran between the rocks, the water was clear and clean, the rocks beneath it visible and shining through the water. It was narrow enough to step over and on the opposite side was enough space to leave horses and let them drink freely from the stream. The only way back out of the small ravine was the way they had come, or along the path of the stream.

Nash ran a hand down the buckskins neck, patting her gently, then he began to remove the saddle and bridle. She wanted to dip her head into the inviting stream but stood obediently while buckles were freed, and the saddle was lifted from her back. Nash noted that the woman was doing the same for Ted's horse, her quick fingers finding the buckles, releasing them, and her confident manner, and instructions to the horse made it stand while she did. When the bridle was gone and the saddle pulled from her back the horses moved to the stream, standing side by side, their necks bent and taking in lengthy draughts of the cool clear water.

Nash pulled a coarse bristled brush from his pack and began to run it along her flanks where the saddle had been, rubbing away sweat and dirt. After a dozen strokes, he pulled away the gathered strands of hair caught in the bristles and let them drift from his hand on the light breeze running through the ravine. Then he began again, his hands running along the horse in a smooth slow motion, pressing away the dust from the ride that had gathered in her coat.

"Have you another brush?" Lucy said, gesturing to Ted's horse.

Nash shook his head. "You can have this one when I've finished. Mind you, Nantai, won't let me finish before she's done."

"The horse won't let you finish?" Lucy asked, confused.

"No ma'am, she won't," Nash stopped mid-way through a brush stroke along her back and stood back, almost immediately the buckskin's head swung round towards him, her nostrils flaring, and she snorted at him. Nash, chuckling, began brushing again. "She's carried me all day, ma'am, it's the least I can do. Long rides like this and it's easy to give her a sore back. We got an understanding. She'll look after me and I'll look after her."

"Uncle Clem was good with horses, he'd break them, sell some to the Apache, and if they had injuries, they'd bring them to him sometimes," the woman said, then as if it explained everything she added, "he was from Donegal in Ireland."

Nash nodded in reply, and he continued with the rhythmic brushing, it wasn't just for the horse. Nash found that after a long day in the saddle the motion helped to free his own muscles, loosening a tight back, and he'd sleep better for it. Swapping sides, he began to remove the dust from the other side of the buckskin.

"She's a mighty fine horse, sir," Lucy said. "Uncle Clem said Buckskins were like the cobs he'd rode in Ireland, except they are piebald and black and white, with longer mains, but the same strong legs and muscles."

"Thank you, ma'am, I've seen a few of those horses that have been brought over, but they don't fare as well with the heat, their coats are too thick. I guess it's colder where they are from," Nash had moved on to the horse's mane, first running his fingers through it to separate the strands before applying the brush. When he was satisfied, he moved to her tail, again pulling the strands apart and removing some snippets of grass and sagebrush that had become caught before running the brush through it.

When he was finished Nash held the brush towards the woman. "She's happy now."

Sure, enough the buckskin didn't turn its head again, instead she shook her head rearranging her mane and twitched her tail, seemingly satisfied with Nash's work.

Lucy took the brush and began to brush Ted's horse down. He'd not tended to it since they'd left, and the bristles clogged straight away with dirt and loose fur. For a moment Nash thought to say that by rights, she should leave the work for Ted, but then he thought better of it. It would take her a while, and after what she had been through the task would be a help, she was doing a good job and he could leave her be for a while.

Nash opened his pack and strapped on a second gun belt; he took from within a soft roll of cloth a matched pair of Colt .44's, and inserted one into each holster. The old single shot he pushed into the front of his belt.

"That's quite a difference," Lucy said from where she was still brushing down Ted's horse.

"Can't be too careful, ma'am," Nash said smiling.

There was a sudden noise from the bank they had descended down, as several pebbles were dislodged, and rolled and bounced down to land plopping in the stream. Nash looked up, descending the bank was Ted. Nash cursed silently. Lucy had also seen him and stopped mid brush stroke.

"Stay here, ma'am," Nash said.

On strong muscled legs, Nash, bounded up the bank towards Ted, meeting him when he was half-way down.

"What have you seen?" Nash said quickly, grasping Ted's arm.

A look of confusion clouded Ted's face for a moment. "Nothin' out there to worry about. I've a thirst on me like a desert rat, you could have brought me some water up?"

Nash roughly released his arm. "Go down, I'll take the watch. Where's the Henry?"

Ted was already moving down the bank towards the stream and called over his shoulder. "Up top, on the ridge."

Nash uttered another curse, this time it wasn't silent, and made his way up the bank as quickly as he could. The gun was where Ted had left it and Nash took it up, cradling it in his arms as he slowly scanned the horizon. There was little to see, nothing moved. There were no birds in the air, no trails of smoke, no faint whisps of dust rising from the hooves of horses. The land was silent of the noises of man, the only sounds those from the crickets and the occasional buzz of an insect, and then from behind him the pad of a dog's paws on the dust.

Rock emerged from the brush, his broken ear was floppy, the fur along his back flat, and his muscles relaxed. The dog also wasn't aware of anyone near their camp.

The top of the ridge gave a good view of the land below. When Ted came back up, he'd send him back for water and his pack. They could bed down near the horses, but he knew he'd have to take the night watch on his own, he couldn't trust Ted. And he didn't yet know how he felt about the woman, Lucy, either.

There were three of them now, they had a long way to travel and only two horses. She didn't weigh much, but she was riding behind his saddle, and it wasn't good for Nantai's back. It'd be better to share the ride between the two horses. Their route had changed now, and he did know of a ranch, a small outpost owned by Arch Gadster, he usually had horses to trade, and more. Nash didn't like Arch, he was a man to be wary of, but it might be that he could buy a horse for Lucy from him, although he doubted if the price would be a fair one. Nash, settled back, the Henry, across his chest, the weight a comfort, his hat tipped forward he settled back to listen to the sounds of the evening and wait for Ted to return.

Rock arrived first, circling the top of the ridge three times before choosing where he would spend the night. He lay down closer to the edge of the ridge, he had a better view of the land below than Nash did, and that was just fine.

It was hours before Ted returned, and Nash listened to his noisy ascent up the bank from the stream hearing every step, every dislodged pebble bounce down the bank, every grunt and huff that Ted uttered as he made his way clumsily back to the ridge.

"Howdy," Nash said when Ted finally emerged on the ridge.

"It's a harder climb back up in the dark," Ted announced.

Nash let his eyes wander over the other man and sighed. He'd not thought to bring back water or Nash's pack. Rising smoothly Nash handed Ted the Henry. "I'll get my pack and take the first watch."

"There's no-one can see us down there," Ted pointed back down to where the horses and Lucy were, "surely it's safe enough for us all down there."

Nash cast his eyes in the direction Ted had pointed. "That might be so, but if someone does notice us then we'll be like pigs in a pen and easy to slaughter."

Ted shrugged. "Yeah, but they have to come along this ridge first to see us."

"And I'll be here to make sure they don't," Nash said stepping past Ted and heading down the slope to retrieve his pack.

He was back five minutes later, his pack over his shoulder, and arrived silently back at the top of the ridge, his appearance making Ted jump.

"Have a care! I didn't hear you coming," Ted said, then for the first time he seemed to notice the colts. "Hey, where's the Perry gone?"

Nash grinned. "Felt like I might need a bit more firepower now we've tripped over an Indian nest."

Ted glanced down as his single .44 sourly.

# CHAPTER SEVEN

Nash didn't bother to wake Ted to take over the watch from him, there was no trusting the man to watch his back, and so Nash decided that night he'd need to watch his own. He was joined in the morning by Lucy and Ted.

Opening his pack, he took out the tin of coffee and set it on the ground before pulling out the jerky. Rock was watching him closely.

"Ma'am, you just watch that dog, it don't look it, but it's a vicious cur, and Nash rightly tells me it likes no one except him," Ted said, seating himself a good distance from the dog.

Lucy, ignoring Ted, asked. "You've a tin of coffee there, sir, do you want me to make some. Uncle Clem said I made the best coffee in the state."

Nash smiled. "Thank you, ma'am, and I'm sure you do. But today we'll do without the fire."

Lucy blushed. "Of course, sir, that was a foolish thought."

Ted rushed to her defense. "It was a kindly offer. Nash is just being overly cautious, after the miles we put in yesterday I doubt there is anyone close behind us."

Nash looked at Ted, thought about telling him that the Apache would ride through the night, if the going became poor then one would sleep on the horse while another led them, so they could still make progress. That the braves were hardened to live in this land, it neither made them afraid, nor nervous, they were at home in the dust and the heat and driven by a very different kind of heart than the one that beat in Ted's chest. But it would serve little purpose, and it might upset the woman, not that he was bothered too much about that, but if she got all teary the way women did sometimes and started crying it would make the journey harder. It was something Nash could do without.

Ted pulled out his jerky and offered some to Lucy.

"This is very good, sir," she said.

Ted grinned. "Glad you like it ma'am, it was the best they had."

Nash, chewing on his own slowly, didn't comment. Rock slunk across the camp and settled himself down next to Nash.

"Are you going to give him some," Ted said, gesturing towards the dog.

"It's not good to feed a dog on the trail," Nash replied slowly.

Ted offered Lucy more jerky, then pointing towards Rock he said, "He's askin' real nice."

"He can ask all he likes," Nash said, he'd finished eating and was packing the remaining jerky in his pack.

"Well, I think you're being kind of mean, and that's sayin' something as he bit me real bad," Ted said raising his still bound injured wrist.

Nash didn't want to say more, but Rock was watching Ted closely. "There's plenty out there he can find to eat. All you'd be doing by feeding him is dullin' his appetite, and then he'll not hunt. You're not doin' him no favors. And remember what happened last time you fed him."

Ted cast a piece of jerky towards the dog. He didn't make to throw it like last time, but carefully tossed it towards the Rock. Nash scowled, no doubt Ted thought he was impressing the woman.

"It's a few small bits, my old Pa always said the way to a dog's heart was through its stomach. I told you I had a way with dogs," Ted said, grinning.

Nash didn't answer. His gaze for a moment was on the piece of jerky that lay in the dust. Rock's eyes weren't on it, his broken ear had lurched forwards and his nose was scenting the air.

"We got trouble," Nash said quietly.

Ted made to rise.

"Stay down, stay still," Nash warned.

Rock turned towards Nash, and silently he motioned for the dog to leave. Rock didn't rush from the ridge, but slowly disappeared down the slope.

"What do we do now?" Ted said nervously.

"Wait, Rock'll be back soon enough. Do you know how to use that piece you've been carrying with you?" Nash asked Ted.

"Sure, I do," Ted said, patting the holster with his palm.

"Good, well let's hope you don't need to prove that," Nash said, then turning towards Lucy he said, "Ma'am, go back down the slope and wait with the horses, it'll be safer that way. No place up here for a woman."

Lucy nodded, and quietly descended from the ridge back to where the horses were tethered. She did so quietly, Nash noted, without the cussing and scrabbling noises that came from Ted when he clambered up and down with all the grace of a three-legged steer.

"I can't hear nothing," Ted said switching his position to ease a cramp in his leg.

"If you don't quit twisting about like that someone else is going to hear something," Nash warned under his breath.

Ted ignoring him, continued. "Where's that damned dog of yours gone?"

"He'll be back when he's ready," Nash said.

"You sure he's not gone off and killed a coyote? And we're hunkering up here in the damned sun while he sleeps it off," Ted continued, an edge of a whine creeping into his voice.

"I'm sure," Nash replied firmly.

"How are you, though?" Ted wasn't going to let this rest.

"There was a mighty tasty piece of jerky right in front of his nose, and he ignored it, it's still there, there's only one thing that'll put that dog off his food," Nash said.

"What's that then?" Ted asked.

"Trouble. Now quiet down," Nash warned.

Ted, his heels in the ground pushed himself backwards so he could rest against a rock, it was more comfortable Nash was sure, but now the damn fool couldn't see over the edge of the ridge to the land below.

Hearing was like night sight, once you'd seen a flame then it was gone, and Nash knew that listening to Ted's shuffles and complaints had stopped him listening to the more distant noises from the plains. Tipping his hat forwards for a moment he closed his eyes and tried to take in the sounds around him, he heard the noise of a pebble grating under foot on a rock almost too late.

Snapping his eyes open Nash could see the profile of the ridge a dozen steps before him broken by the outline of two braves. The sun was behind them, and Nash knew in an instant they'd been seen.

Hauling the Henry up, the gun primed and ready, he fired. The explosion was met with a scream. A plume of smoke obscured them for a moment, then the breeze rounded it up and it was pulled from the ridge top. There was a shot from his right, but Ted had missed, the brave was now halfway between his fallen comrade and Nash, a gun in his hand, Nash fired without hesitation, the shot caught the man in the chest, and lifted him from his feet, sending him backwards away from Nash, his dead hand released the gun and it span end over end and landed clattering on the stones.

"Take the right," Nash said to Ted, retrieving the fallen gun, he spun the barrel, it was loaded. For the first time he looked at Ted.

Ted, his body shaking like a leaf in a gale, lay on the ground. If there was a scream of terror or one of pain it couldn't make it out of his constricted throat. Blood was pumping from his left thigh, the hole small where the bullet had entered but on the opposite side where it had left there was a gaping wound, white bone splinters had been forced through the flesh and clothing.

There was no time to help.

On his belly Nash made it to the edge of the ridge, below were horses and more braves, two were skirting around to bring an attack from behind and two more coming straight up towards him. With the Henry he took two shots towards the pair rounding the ridge then two more at those coming straight up towards them. The brave on the right, hit in the center of his chest reeled backwards, dead.

Nash scrambled back to Ted where he lay dying. He'd shot through his own leg as he tried to pull the gun from the holster. "I cannot get you off here, and you're gunna bleed out. You've blood pouring from you like a split barrel. I'll not leave you to them."

A flicker of hope rested for a moment on Ted's pale face. Ted's gun was still in the holster, Nash pulled it free, and he met the suddenly wide terrified eyes of the younger man. Nash didn't hesitate and pulled the trigger.

Nash ran down the ridge, his boots sliding in the rock and dust, there was no need to be quiet now.

"Well done, ma'am," Nash said, both horses were saddled and ready. Nash slapped Ted's horse's rump, sending it to climb back to the ridge, he chased it to make sure the horse would continue and not come back down.

Running back a moment later he was in his saddle hauling Lucy up behind him.

"Where's Ted?"

"He ain't coming ma'am," was all Nash said as he pulled the buckskin into the narrow stream and set her along the stream bed for as long as he dared. When it got too deep, and he felt she was going to fall or trap a hoof, he let her bound back up onto the bank and from there they made their way from the campsite.

There were no more sounds of shots from behind him. Nash had not once bothered to look back to see if they were being pursued. If he was being followed, then a glance over his shoulder wasn't going to change that fact. He concentrated instead on getting them as far away from the danger as he could.

# CHAPTER EIGHT

They had ridden for hours when they came across the homestead, it was tucked away into a vee in the valley side, unless you approached it head on it was hard to find, and even then, the walls blended with the rocky terrain around it. It was humble, weathered and it's remains stood as testament to the resilience and perseverance of those who had built it and called it home. But it was a sign of life, and the only one they had seen all day. Ted slowed Nantai as they approached, the Henry ready.

"Howdy," he called when they were not too close.

No reply.

The desert wind whipped the buckskin's tail and mane and produced poor musical notes from the rusted wire fencing, but apart from that there was just silence. Nash nudged the horse forward, calling a greeting once more.

Dropping from the saddle and helping Lucy down, he said. "Hold Nantai here, ma'am while I take a look around."

It was abandoned, the left-hand wall had crumbled, and the roof was gone. Burnt a long while ago, but the scorch marks still lay on the white walls. It had been no more than a one room cabin, the roof timbers, burnt, lay on the inside, along with part of the wall that had collapsed, but the three remaining walls still provided some shelter from the scorching sun. That a family had chosen here to call home seemed hard to imagine. The land around would have been hard to farm, but there was evidence of their efforts.

A dilapidated fence, made of sagging wooden posts and rusty wire, encircled the homestead. And nearby a ramshackle barn leaned precariously, its walls patched with scraps of salvaged wood and metal. The barn's roof, repaired with tattered tarps and old blankets, barely held back the elements, and huge sections had been torn open by the unforgiving desert winds.

Walking back, he took Nantai's reins from Lucy. "We'll bed down in there, there's a storm coming in and it'll serve us well."

Lucy had seen the dark clouds rolling towards them, and felt the breeze increase in ferocity, by the time they had led Nantai into the barn it had begun to hammer the remains of the roof, flapping tarpaulins and tugging at walls and roof.

"If you don't mind, ma'am, can you take the saddle off Nantai for me, and I'll scout around for water," Nash asked.

"I don't mind at all, sir," Lucy said, taking the reins from him.

The reason the homestead was here was soon obvious right behind it, rising from the rocks was a spring. It bubbled to the surface and a manmade cistern had been cut into the rocks around it. The men who had lived here had built an enclosure around it and capped it with a wooden lid to stop it disappearing in the summer heat. The wooden lid was held down with a small cairn of rocks, Nash moved them and pulled away the lid, below it was sweet clean water. The pool was a good foot deep, and it extended sideways under the rock, a man-made cistern.

Lying flat he lowered his head inside and waited. It took time to adjust your eyes to darkness, for them to be able to see the small details in the gloom. Nash waited, there was a slight draught of cooler air rising from beneath the boards and washing over his face, and the air carried with it a damp earthy smell.

"What you doing?" It was Lucy's voice.

Nash didn't rise, but keeping his head inside the cistern replied, his words having an unearthly echo. "Always wise, ma'am, to make sure the waters fresh."

Nash heard Lucy's feet shuffling the dried earth as she moved closer, but she didn't speak again.

Slowly the interior of the cistern began to come into view. He could see the tool marks in the rock, small angular dents, line upon line of them showing where the cistern had been hollowed out from the living rock. He'd seen the like before in caves, they were the tool marks made by the ancients, the cistern had been here for a long time.

In his right hand he held a pale-yellow rock, lowering his arm he released it and immediately heard the splash as it entered the water, his eyes able to watch it as it sank. The water wasn't deep, the cistern seemed extended out under the rock sideways, it smelt fresh enough. Satisfied Nash pushed himself back up smoothly, replaced the board and rebuilt the small cairn.

"There's plenty of water, and it's clean and fresh," Nash said as he placed the last rock on top of the pile.

There was no bucket to be seen, Nash filled the two canteens he had over his shoulder and headed back, his eyes roving the remains of the homestead for a bucket to fill for Nantai. He found none.

When he came back to the barn Lucy had cleared the floor of debris, she said. "If you found water there's a stone trough there, I've got most of the sand from it."

Cut from stone, the trough was at the back of the barn. Nash looked sadly at the two canteens, they would hold just enough to wet the bottom and no more. But his horse needed water, and in the absence of a bucket he knew he had no choice. Taking his hat off he filled it from the canteen and held it before the buckskin's nose. Nantai drank carefully, and Nash filled it four more times before he took water from the canteen for himself.

"Is that enough for her?" Lucy asked, coming to stand close to the horse's head.

"No, ma'am, but it'll take the edge off for her while I fill that trough. See you get a drink yourself," Nash said already heading back with the canteens.

The storm was pulling in closer, and it took him an hour of return trips to fill the trough a third full, satisfied that the buckskin had enough for her thirst he relented and sat down next to Lucy. The noise from the wind hammering on the roof had intensified, and the erratic banging from above made it hard to talk.

"I don't think we'll get much sleep," Lucy said smiling.

"That maybe a good thing," Nash replied, then he said. "Might be quieter in the old homestead, I'll leave Nantai in here."

The pair crossed from the noisy barn to the crumbling homestead. There was silence between them for a while and then Lucy spoke. "What happened to your friend, Ted?"

Nash considered this for a moment. He wasn't one given over to lying ordinarily. "They came from behind us and in front at the same time, Ted fired off an' hit one square in the chest, lifted him clean off his feet, but he took a shot from behind."

Lucy nodded, then turning her mind to practicalities said. "I shouldn't have put his pack on his horse really."

Nash shrugged. "You weren't to know, and you can be sure those braves will have seen it. That horse will have been chased down by now, so making it a might more tempting probably turned their minds from us for a while."

Lucy paled. "You think they'll come after us again?"

"They followed us from where your uncle was killed, so I guess so. Musta' spotted us and followed," Nash said thoughtfully.

Lucy looked down at her feet. "I'm sorry, this is my fault. If I hadn't tripped and fired that shot, they wouldn't have known you were there."

Nash was silent for a moment, then said. "Apache have a saying, ma'am, and it's true. The past is made of stone, no point trying to change it."

Lucy looked up and met his eyes, her own were wet along the bottoms with tears that threatened to spill down her cheeks, with the back of her hand she angrily brushed them away. "That's very kind of you to say so, sir."

"You did tell me that your Uncle Clem said you fixed the best coffee in the state, with this storm coming in it'll hide a little smoke. If you'd be kind enough to make some, ma'am, I'd appreciate it," Nash said smiling.

"I'd be mighty pleased to, sir," Lucy replied, smiling.

Nash took the coffee from his pack, along with a flint and steel before he propped himself against the door frame of the old homestead, one eye on the approaching storm, standing in the soft glow of twilight, his silhouette framed against the vast, open landscape. Lucy scavenged around the homestead, methodically gathering twigs and kindling. With a dried piece of sagebrush, she swept a clear space in the middle of the floor and began deftly arranging the wood into a tepee shape as Nash watched. The flickering light of the setting sun casting long shadows as she struck the steel, the spark caught, and soon a flame was dancing to life in the light evening breeze. Crackling softly, the fire grew, illuminating the soft contours of her face as she blew on the dry brush, breathing life into the fire.

How old was she, Nash wondered? Her eyes were on the task before her, and this was the first time he had truly looked at her. Beneath the dirt on her face and the desert dust was a skin that told of an age close to twenty. Her hair, sun-kissed, was tied, and hung down her back in a lose braid. Her shirt was a man's, too long and shapeless, hiding her body, and below that the pants. In the towns you never saw womenfolk dressed like that, but Nash saw plenty on his travels who had abandoned skirts in the name of practicality. On the homesteads, farms and ranches he guessed there were none there to judge them save their own family, and it would be a fool that did not accept that trying to ride, hunt and ranch in petticoats was a folly. He guessed she'd have woman's clothing for best, and she would have been working with the uncle she kept talking about when the Indians attacked.

The warmth of the fire began to radiate, contrasting with the cool night air, and the sounds of the wilderness surrounding them. Nash leaned back against the door frame, content to watch as the fire crackled and the sparks rose into the darkening sky from the roofless homestead.

In front of Lucy, a small pot hung over the flames. Lucy had found some lengths of wire, twisted them to form an arch over the flames, and from it a small pot hung. Lucy carefully measured out coffee grounds, pouring them into the pot with a practiced hand. The aroma of brewing coffee began to mingle with the dry scent of the plains. As the coffee bubbled and steamed, Lucy occasionally stirred it with a stick, waiting patiently for it to reach the perfect brew.

Lucy glanced around, catching Nash's eye, she smiled. "Just a few more minutes."

When she was satisfied, she poured some into a tin cup and brought it to him, holding it out.

Nash took the cup. "Thank you, ma'am, smells real nice."

Lucy returned to the fire, waiting for the pot to cool enough so she could drink from it.

Nash took a moment to savor the simple pleasure of a hot drink in the great outdoors. Taking a sip, he smiled towards her. "Uncle Clem was right; you make good coffee."

Lucy smiled and dropped to sit cross legged before the fire, the pot, now a little cooler, balanced on one knee.

They slept inside the walls of the homestead, the night stars framed above them by the remains of the walls. The fire was damped down, and the only light came from above, a half-moon sending a cool light towards them until it was obscured by the storm clouds.

"So where were you boys heading?" Lucy asked, breaking the silence.

Nash looked round but didn't answer straight away, and Lucy, thinking she'd been presumptuous in asking said quickly. "Sorry, sir, it's not my business to ask. I was just trying to make conversation."

Nash smiled. "I don't mind you asking, it's the answer I was having trouble with. I don't rightly know where I'm heading anymore."

Lucy looked puzzled, and Nash continued. "I was taking Ted to Bakersfield; he had a claim back in Oatman he wanted to register. I knew the trail, taken it a time or two in the past myself, so I was just guiding him there."

"So after ...." Lucy paused as she searched for the right words. "After what happened today there's no need to go to Bakersfield."

Nash nodded.

"Did he have family in Oatman?" Lucy asked.

"None that he told me about. He'd not long since come from Ireland, said he'd come over on his own" Nash said.

Lucy nodded. "So, no need to go back to Oatman."

Nash shook his head. Not about to tell her that there were a few other reasons why he'd be keeping clear of Oatman. "Is there anywhere I can take you, ma'am."

Lucy was silent for a moment. "Uncle Clem was taking us to his brother's ranch, it's down near Goldsprings. I think that's where I'm going to be heading, and you?"

"Goldsprings sounds as good a place as any, ma'am," Nash replied, smiling.

"Sir, I didn't mean that you should take me. It's an awful imposition," Lucy said quickly.

"I've nowhere else I plan to go, so Goldsprings is as good as anywhere, Northwest of here if my memory is right. And in all honesty, ma'am, I can hardly leave you here. If you keep fixing the coffee and cooking some meat when I've the occasion to find some, then I'd be happy to take you," Nash said.

Lucy blushed. "I am grateful, sir."

They fell into a companionable silence after that. Goldsprings was as good a place as any to head. Nash just liked moving, he'd been doing it for a long time. It wasn't the destination that mattered, that was just the direction you were going, it was the journey. He knew the town as well; he'd been there a time or two before. He'd take the woman to Goldsprings, then from there find some other place to head to maybe join a cattle drive, maybe just head out on his own towards the coast or Mexico. It didn't really matter where.

Nash knew the storm was coming, he always slept lightly, and when the air shifted and a sense of foreboding came with the increase in persistence of the wind, he rose and went out in the night, bringing Nantai through the door into the sanctuary of the homestead. Lucy had stirred as he tied the mare up at the back of the broken room, but seeing what he was doing had closed her eyes and returned quickly to sleep.

Nash had seen the wall of dust rising in the distance before night fell. The once calm breeze gave way to winds, whipping through the sagebrush and rattling the remnants of the homestead. The sky above them was no longer pin-pricked with stars but black, and the distant rumbling of thunder echoed across the plains.

Nash made sure the fire was doused, knowing that the winds would revive the embers and scatter them around the inside of the homestead. He checked his gear was secure, and hefted it a little closer into a corner, and tugged the leather straps on his pack tighter, storm dust could get by just about anything. He was suddenly thankful for the shelter of the crumbling homestead, the few wooden beams that were left creaking ominously in the wind. There was a sudden lull in the wind, a moment of silence, and Nash suddenly realized he had underestimated the intensity of the storm.

Reaching down he grabbed Lucy's arm and pulled her towards the wall beneath the missing window. A moment later the first gusts hit, bringing with them a swirl of sand and debris that stung their skin and obscured their vision. The wind forced sand through the missing door, scouring the ragged frame and it flew through the missing window above their heads. The tempest grew closer as the storm unleashed its fury.

Words were pointless, the wind would tear them away before they could be heard. Crammed into the corner of the old homestead, a blanket pulled over their heads and pinned tightly down with hands and boots they waited.

Then sheets of rain began to fall, lashing against the ground and creating small rivers in the parched earth all around them. They both huddled against the wall of the homestead, listening to the violent howl of the wind and the crack of lightning illuminating the sky, the bright light strong enough to piece even the wool of the blanket. Water poured down the walls, ran down their backs and ponded on the homestead floor. Where there had been dust there was now a fine slurry of mud.

As the storm raged closer Nash could feel the adrenaline surging through him. Afterall, he'd been named for a storm, his mother had called him na'ashjii. There was something about them, their intensity and unpredictability, that spoke to him.

He'd been through storms before, but each one brings its unique intensity and unpredictability. The wind howled like a wild animal, and the air was thick with the scent of rain and earth, mingling with the dry dust that had been stirred up. Above them was only blackness, until the bright arcs of lightning lit up the boiling dark clouds for a moment, highlighting the remains of the blackened beams and the ragged tops of the walls. It was followed quickly by the sound of thunder, rolling towards them like the sound of a giant's drum, it seemed to shake the ground they sat on.

The wind picked up, forcing its way inside the homestead and finding inside brush wood, dust, grit and the remains of the roof to toss against the walls. A bolt of lightning lit the interior, and he found himself looking into the alarmed eyes of Nantai. Squeezing Lucy's arm, he ducked from under the blanket and felt the full force of the wind, laden with rain and he was wet to his skin in moments.

He smoothed a hand down the buckskin's neck, his words of reassurance were ripped from his lips by the gale before they reached Nantai's ears, and he knew they were wasted, but he spoke them anyway. The horse turned her head towards him, resting it on his shoulder, her eyes closed and together they stood and bore the brunt of the gale as it burst its way through the doorway. The rain continued to fall in sheets, creating a symphony of sound as it pelted the walls and then cracked on the hard earth floor.

When the storm eventually waned, and the gusts stopped forcing him forward against the horse he left her and slid down the wall next to where the woman was. His hat pulled down hard, he tried to snatch some sleep from the remainder of the night.

It was safe.

For the moment.

If the braves were out there still, they'd be hunkered down against the storm as well, he knew that, and they'd also be taking advantage of the break to sleep, even if it was only for a short while.

The dawn was grey, and the clouds were still storm ridden and bruised from the night. Rising, Nash stretched, crossed the small room and reassured the buckskin, before stepping through the doorway. Outside, the landscape was transformed. The once-dry plains were now a swirling sea of mud and water, and the scent was fresh and vibrant, and the air still prickled with the intensity of the storm.

# CHAPTER NINE

Nash untied his pack and flipped back the leather cover. The contents were thankfully dry. Unwrapping the telescope, he put the dry cover back safely inside the pack and leaning against the door frame of the homestead slowly worked his way along the horizon.

"See anything?" Lucy asked, coming to stand beside him.

Nash finished running the scope over the landscape before he lowered it and shook his head. "Doesn't mean much."

"After last night there'll be no tracks for them to follow," Lucy waved her arm towards the mud and sand outside of the homestead. It was a terrain of rapidly drying puddles, the ground, where the water had already evaporated was evenly pock marked by the rain.

Nash too was looking at the land around them. "True, but when we leave here that's going to be a whole different story, ma'am."

For a moment Lucy didn't seem to comprehend his words, her eyes running over the fresh wind and rain cleaned plains, then she realized what he meant, and her hand flew to her chest. "Dear Lord. What do we do?" Lucy said, turning to face him.

"We are stopping here until the ground firms or we'll be leaving a trail that'll be cast in the ground from now until we get another storm like that," Nash said, then added, "Find what wood you can and prop it against the walls outside to dry, I'll see what else these poor folk left us."

Water they now had. The wood covered cistern at the back of the homestead was full. The folk who had made it long ago knew the value of water and the cistern they had cut into the rock was large. Behind the remains of the barn and running along the edge of the rocky rise was buffalo grass, it had already soaked up the moisture from the storm and stems bristled a little stronger in their stumpy clumps. It would provide Nantai with grazing along the ridge, buckskins were fastidious grazers, their front teeth were not prevented from reaching the bottom of the buffalo grass by a large nose, and they were perfectly designed to make the most of very little.

Nash tethered his mare behind the remains of the barn, she'd be out of sight of the plains. He fetched her water and when he was happy, he began his search for whatever else the place could offer. Close to where the water was, their roots living from the moisture in the soil thereabouts was a tangle of edible plants, squaw cabbage, lambs' quarters and even some dandelion greens sprouting between the buffalo grass. Further in was a cutting into the cliff face, wind, rain and ice over the years had cleaved the opening in the rock, but they had also forced in soil and blown in seeds and the bottom was home to more plants.

Nash smiled and twisted the top from some zea maize. Using his thumbs he forced away the outside covering to reveal below the pale-yellow kernels. It smelt good and it was ripe. There was at least a dozen within easy reach, he plucked six and left the rest, taking them back to the homestead.

"I found these, and there's squaw cabbage, and some other greens behind the homestead," Nash said, holding out the tops from the maze.

Lucy took the offered maze, her own fingers pressing away the leaves, and smiling she said. "Can I light a cooking fire?"

Nash shook his head, he peeled back the leaves and sunk his teeth into the kernels. Nourished by the water that seeped into the gorge and protected from the worst rays of the sun, the maze was as sweet as an apple. Lucy joined him, Nash shared a little jerky between them, and they drank cool water from the cistern. It was enough and that dry nag in the pit of his stomach, the annoying distraction of hunger was soon gone.

"A feast," Lucy said, wiping the back of her hand across her mouth.

Nash smiled. "There's more maize. I guess that's what the folks who were here were trying to grow, and some of it is still rooting behind the house. I thought of leaving it where it was until we wanted it. We can hole up here for a few days until the ground firms and then head out."

"Do you think they might find us before then?" Lucy asked, her eyes flicking nervously towards the open doorway, and onwards across the empty plains.

Nash shrugged. "They might. How many were there when you and your uncle were attacked?"

"I'd say eight," Lucy replied after a moment.

"So, seven now, but there's only one of me," Nash said.

"I know, you can't fight seven on your own," Lucy lamented.

Nash smiled. "I wasn't even considering fighting them, ma'am, I'm hoping to stay a step ahead, that's all we need to be. And that means out thinking seven Indians, and that's a mighty big ask."

"Uncle Clem said they've not the learning nor the letters. He never thought they were smart," Lucy said.

Nash looked at her, his eyes cold. "I don't mean to sound cruel, ma'am, but I've always thought it's best not to underestimate anyone until you've a full reckoning of them."

"Are you saying that's why Uncle Clem was killed? Because he underestimated them?" Nash's words had definitely touched a nerve, three days of anger of poor sleep, being beaten by the storm and the horror were about to boil to the surface.

"Ma'am," Nash said slowly. "My mother's name was Tazhi, it means strong woman, and she was Apache."

Lucy just gawped at him. "You're Indian?"

Nash smiled. “Not pure, ma’am, though sometimes I wish I was. My Pappy was from Georgetown.”

Lucy was studying his face. Now he’d told her he could see that she was picking out those features that he’d inherited from his mother. The nose slightly hooked, his skin darkened by the sun was naturally a duskier shade than her own and his hair, hidden beneath his hat was dark and black as a crow’s wing.

Nash smiled. “I been told a time or two I take after my father, rather than my mother.”

“I don’t understand?” Lucy said haltingly.

“What is there to understand, ma’am. When a man and a woman love each other there’s seldom anything that can come between them, and that’s how it was. They met at a trading post and ran away together, and I’d be around five before she met her family again after my father died,” Nash explained openly.

“Oh, my word, so you really do know the Indians well,” Lucy said, her eyes wide.

“I wish I knew more, I spent six years there, then my grandmother persuaded my mother that she could give me a better life, and I grew up with her on a plantation in the south near Charlotte,” Nash said, “She’d inherited it from her father and if I’d stayed it might have been mine.”

“And you didn’t stay there?” Lucy said, shocked.

Nash shook his head. "I'd no liking to make my way in the world on the backs of other men. She had other grandchildren who cared less, so I wasn't missed."

Lucy looked at him strangely. "You just turned your back on a plantation?"

"I did," Nash said, "My Grandmother was happy, we got along, she didn't like being there either overly much. She was from London in England, and she'd have given anything to go back there. But she made the best of what there was. So, she understood me when I wanted to leave."

Lucy shook her head. "I can't understand why you'd leave so much."

"I've been plenty happy since, ma'am," Nash replied simply.

From behind the house came the sound of pebbles skittering down the rock face. Nash held a palm towards Lucy indicating she should stay where she was, and quickly he lifted the Henry from against the wall where it rested. Rising slowly, taking careful steps, and listening for any further rockfalls, Nash slid silently from the broken front door of the homestead. When he reached the corner, he waited. The sound of claws on stone reached him but before he had time to glance around the corner of the wall a furry head with a broken ear appeared.

Nash smiled. Propping the gun against the wall he dropped to his knees, wrapped his arms around the dog and rested his head for a moment on the top of the dogs. "Dii," he said in Apache.

Nash received a rough lick up on one side of his face. Patting the dog, he led him into the homestead and for a moment busied himself providing the animal with water. Rock drank from the pot noisily and messily, half of each great gulp of water seemed to eject itself from the sides of the dog's mouth and every few moments he'd turn to observe Nash, the water running from his mouth.

Nash shook his head. "His only fault, ma'am, he's mighty wasteful with water. It's a good job we don't have a shortage."

"Where do you think he's been?" Lucy asked.

"He'll have found himself somewhere safe during the storm, and he's an Indian dog so tracking us would not have been hard," Nash said, ruffling the fur on the dog's head again and making the broken ear wobble.

Nash had the scope in his hand again, slowly he surveyed the plains beyond the homestead. "There's more rain coming in, ma'am, not as bad as before, but it'll cover the smell of a fire if you'd like to light one. Some of your coffee would be very welcome."

Lucy smiled.

Nash kept watch even when Lucy gave him a cup of hot coffee. "I'll cook us up some corn as well and add in those greens you told me about."

"Thank you, ma'am," Nash said smiling.

"I'll see what I can find," Lucy said before disappearing around the back of the homestead.

They ate their meal in silence as the light began to disappear from the sky and Lucy, the blanket wrapped around her, fell asleep before Nash had finished eating. He doused the fire, and after checking Nantai settled himself down as well.

In the morning Nash woke and crouching down he dug his fingers into the earth in front of the homestead. It was still sodden with moisture, it had rained again during the night. Not long, but enough to soak the earth for a second time. Another day or two of sun was needed before they headed out otherwise, they'd be leaving a permanent trail on the earth. Better to stay put until that could be avoided. When he'd awoken Rock was gone, and as Nash was rising the dog padded back round the end of the homestead, the fur around his mouth bloody.

Nash ruffled the dog's ears. "At least one of us has had a good breakfast."

Rock, having had enough of Nash's attentions flapped his head in the way dogs did, making his ears slap against the side of his head then went in search of somewhere to sleep off his meal. Nash watched him go, the dog was relaxed, and it was a good sign. But just to be sure he took out his scope and ran it slowly over the plains.

Nothing moved.

It was empty.

The sun was heating the ground and all along the horizon he could see the hazy blur as she dried the plains. Another day and it would be safe to head out.

Nash moved Nantai further along the ridge so she could reach fresh patches of buffalo grass. There wasn't much to do but sit and wait out the day.

# CHAPTER TEN

When Nash awoke Rock was gone. The dog had lain asleep with its head pillowed on one of Nash's boots. Nash stretched, shifted his hat back a little on his head and pushed himself up. Lucy was asleep on the other side of the homestead.

Nothing moved, the sun was low in the sky, moving towards the doorway, he smiled when he looked at the earth. The sun had done her work, the pock marks from the rain were now baked into the surface of the once wet mud. They'd head out tomorrow, early before sun up.

Rock rounded the corner of the door, his head low, the broken ear twitching. Nash knew immediately that something was wrong. Pulling the scope from his pack he scanned the horizon.

Indians.

They were approaching slowly, through the scope he could clearly see the two in the lead conversing with each other, the one on the right was laughing as he watched them share a joke. And they were heading straight towards the homestead, and Nash knew why.

The cistern at the back had been built long ago, it would have been used by the tribes, a known place to find water and then, foolishly, the homestead had been built next to it.

A claim staked.

Probably innocently enough. There was no-one there, the cistern would have looked abandoned, belonging to a bygone age. But that wasn't the truth. Leave anything on the plains for a few days and dust would cover it making it look unused, the sand would pile up along the edges of the brickwork, coat the wooden planks on the top and frost the rocks that held them down. But Nash knew that it would not have been forgotten about, and no doubt that's where the tension that led to the homestead being burnt out had stemmed from.

Now they were back. Heading towards the water to satisfy their horses, take some rest in the shadow of the cliff, there was no great urgency in their approach.

Not yet anyway.

Nash quickly collapsed the scope and turned towards where Nantia was tethered. He couldn't ride out and outrun them, there was nowhere to conceal the horse, as soon as they arrived at the homestead they'd see the mare grazing. Nash looked quickly back at the advancing group, further away now that his eye was no longer pressed to the cool brass of the scope, but he knew he didn't have long.

Diving into the inside of the homestead, he grabbed his pack. "We've got company coming our way, ma'am, and it ain't the friendly kind."

Lucy was on her feet in a moment, a cloud of dust erupting around her. "What are we going to do?"

Nash smiled. "Outthink them, I hope.

Can't outride them, I doubt both of us can make the climb to the top of the ridge before they arrive, on my own, I can manage it."

"You're going to leave me?" Lucy's voice was high pitched and shook with nerves.

"Not where they'll find you," Nash smiled, reaching for her hand.

"What do you mean?" Lucy let him pull her from the door of the homestead and round the back to where the water cistern was.

"It's not deep, and it's full, the water's filling the pond at the front, they'll not look inside, and even if they do it's damned dark in there," Nash said, already clearing the rock cairn that pinned down the boards over the entrance.

"You want me to get in there?" the panic was rising, and her eyes were wild.

Nash took hold of both of her hands tightly in his. "Ma'am, yes I do."

"I can't. Don't leave me!" Lucy pleaded.

"I'll not leave you; I'll be up there with a gun giving them more to think about than looking inside there for you," Nash pulled her close for a moment, his lips pressed to hers, "trust me, ma'am."

Before she could reply Nash had the top off the cistern and picking her up lowered her in. "It's not deep, you'll be safe in there."

Quickly he put the wood back and replaced the cairn, then with a switch of sagebrush removed any trace of Lucy's footprints from the camp. He didn't care much if they saw his, they'd know soon enough that he was there, but he'd rather they didn't know he had a woman with him.

As the sun began to set, casting a warm golden hue across the landscape, the group of Indian braves closed on the homestead. Their silhouettes stood tall against the vibrant sky. They rode on sturdy, muscular horses, their movements fluid and purposeful. The sound of hooves against the dry earth breaking the stillness of the evening.

There was no doubt now that they were not heading to the homestead. The wooden structure, weathered and worn by years of exposure, offered little in the way of concealment, Nash knew he couldn't remain there much longer. Peeking through a crack in the wall, his eyes narrowed as he watched the braves approach. Nash's expression a mix of apprehension and curiosity, he wanted them to draw closer so he could see them more clearly, but he was acutely aware of the danger in that.

Nash gripped his hat tightly, contemplating his next move, while the flicker of the sun cast long shadows that danced around him, heightening the sense of impending confrontation. He knew it was one he couldn't avoid.

A switch in his hand he rounded the homestead blurring his footprints as he went. Passing the cistern, he called quietly. "Ma'am, quiet now if you please." Hoping his words would reassure her.

Then with the rifle on his back and the guns in his belt he disappeared into the cleft in the cliff and began the climb to the top.

Nash made the ascent quickly. He reached the rock-strewn top before the Indians had arrived at the homestead.

Lying flat he pulled open the scope again and fitted it to his eye. Nash looked first down at the cistern behind the homestead - nothing moved, and the cairn was still in place, so he knew Lucy was still in her watery hiding place. Then swinging the scope forwards, he found the group of braves. They were closer to the homestead than he had anticipated, on the plains it was often hard to tell how fast a man or animal was moving, there were so few features to gauge a reference from.

Nash's expression hardened. It was a color he recognized, burnt copper, the sun picking out highlights in the long hair as it was caught by the breeze and drifted this way and that. A deeper red than auburn and holding the hues of leaves before they fell from the trees. Ted's scalp had been too tempting to leave, and now it was attached the saddle of one of the Indians, a red and shining prize set off brightly against the white of the buckskin, and next to it another, grey and wispy, a prize he had no doubt claimed from Uncle Clem. The body in the fire had been butchered with a knife he was sure before it had burnt.

The sight twisted his stomach. At least it had been cut from Ted when he had no longer been alive. He'd seen men scalped, heard the screaming, begging and howling as their skin was peeled from their skull. A sharpened knife in his right hand and the hair held tight in his left, it took an Indian only two or three cuts to part the scalp from the bone. Then whooping, he'd hold aloft his prize.

If he was kind he'd finish the kill.

It was harder to take a scalp from a living man, and for some this gave the practice the thrill, to hold their victim down, use the knife with skill, ignore the screams and pleas, and prevent them from twisting from their murderous grasp.

And women suffered worse.

The longer hair was an even greater prize, but they'd not take it until they'd finished with their rape though. He'd seen a woman, crawling, naked, blood streaming down her back, one of her ears flapping loose at the side of her head trying futilely to escape.

Nash shook his head and banished the horror from his mind. He'd not let that happen to Lucy. Indeed, he'd not let that happen to any soul if he could help it. Nash returned his attention to the braves, watching them closely. They were well trained, acutely at home on the plains and he knew they'd sense the presence of outsiders soon enough. At the head rode two braves, the rest rode in a lose pack behind. The one on the right suddenly raised his arm and the whole dynamic of the group changed. Men who had been relaxed and riding in companionable accord were now taught with tension. There was no sound, no shout of command but a second later the group split.

The two at the front headed to the left of the homestead, two more to the right and the remaining three headed straight towards the derelict farm.

They rode fast, their bodies low over the buckskins backs, offering as small a target as possible. There were seven. He'd told Lucy all he needed to do was outthink them - but watching them stream in he wasn't so sure. He dare not shoot as they approached, there was far too great a chance he would miss. Until they reached the homestead they were on the limit of the range of his gun. And if Nash was going to make a shot, he wanted it to count.

# CHAPTER ELEVEN

The group of seven had split, those to the left and right he could no longer see, hidden as they were below the cliff. The pair that had ridden flat out towards the homestead were also out of view behind the broken walls. Nash watched. They'd find Nantai soon enough, hobbled further down the cliff tugging at the sparse clumps of buffalo grass – and they would know then that they were not alone.

There was a sudden shout, the words were too far below him to make out, but he knew that they had found the buckskin. Now they'd begin to scour the camp. Nash switched the scope for the Henry and, his head against the side of the gun, he waited. When he pulled the trigger, it would be a clear shot. Not aimed to scare, or warn, it would be aimed to kill.

Seven to six.

And if he could he wanted to place the bullet in the body of the brave who'd ridden the buckskin with the scalps wafting from his pony. He was the leader. Without him the group would falter, or so he hoped. He was likely to be the son of an elder or a chief and the others would not want to return without him.

There was movement to the left, dismounted, one of them was leading his own horse and Nantai towards the homestead, gesturing behind him. Then the search began in earnest.

Nash was on the top of the cliff, he knew he was out of sight, but the compromise was that he was too far back to view all the homestead below, and that included the cistern behind it. The Henry was trained on the area in front of the missing door. He just needed the right man to emerge, pause for a moment and then he would have his shot. He'd not aim for the head, there was too much chance of a miss, instead he'd aim to put his bullet squarely in the middle of the man's back, the damage would be done when the lead exploded from his chest, bursting open his rib cage.

So far, his target had not placed himself in view.

He could hear their voices more clearly now. They'd scoured the area, and apart from the horse, found nothing.

The brave he sought was wearing a white man's shirt. The tails flapping ludicrously behind him, the front unbuttoned and the sleeves rolled up to his elbows. Nash wouldn't have been surprised to find that the shirt belonged to Lucy's Uncle Clem. One of the others had a woman's hat on his head, it was the wrong way round and the plumes and gauze decorated the back of his head.

War and violence seemed to necessitate the taking of trophies. He'd been on battlefields before and seen men scavenging through the dead, taking weapons, hauling dead limbs from coat sleeves, pulling away belts and boots and cramming the hats of the vanquished onto their heads.

Nash had never had the stomach for it. He believed if you'd taken a man's life then that was the end of it. Once you'd removed that precious gift you should take nothing more. That had been his grandfather's teaching. Not all Indians violated the dead. But then you never knew what those braves had been through. What horrors they'd survived, what atrocities they had witnessed committed upon their own mothers.

He'd been raised a Christian soul by his grandmother, and out of a kindness to her he never voiced his lack of faith. If it wavered when he had been a child, it was banished now. If there was a Lord in heaven, he'd surely turned his back on them.

The Indians had a story. If you bring the gods to despair, if you make them close their eyes and turn away you will lose them. Then the darkness will creep over the plains and evil will take root in men's hearts.

It might have been a story to frighten children, but Nash wondered if that's what was happening. Was it evil that had crept into a man and made him take a blade, and cut a man's scalp from his head? It seemed the longer he lived the more horror there was.

The sun had shifted. Nash took his hand from the Henry and reached up to tip his hat forward, shading his eyes. A sudden glare from the sun and he would be blinded and unable to see. He wiped the sweat from his palm on his sleeve before flexing his fingers and returning his solid hold to the stock.

Still the man he sought had not come back into view.

The blue ladies' hat, the broken feathers bouncing came into view over the edge of a wall. It wasn't Nash's target and there wasn't enough to make it a clean shot. There was a good chance the lead would skitter off the wall, at this distance he needed a bigger target. Nash forced himself to lessen the pressure he'd placed on the trigger.

Patience.

They'd finished their search it seemed; he could see his buckskin tethered next to two other horses in front of the homestead. A sudden noise from his left tensed his muscles. They were in the ravine. He might have brushed out the footprints in the dust but there was no disguising the broken stems and crushed plants in the ravine. They'd know he'd been there and they'd as likely be looking to find another way up. If would be far too risky to climb up in his footsteps and meet a loaded gun as they crested the top.

Then he heard a noise he'd dreaded. A rattle of stones, the dull grate as they were pulled from the wood on the top of the cistern.

There was no time to wait for his Indian in shirt tails to show himself. He had no choice and crawled closer to the edge, careful not to send small stones skittering down over.

He could see four of them. The cairn was gone already, and one had his hands around the edge of the wooden planking and was about to lift it.

Nash took a breath.

Held it.

And fired.

The retort rebounded from the hard ground below, the sound flung back up towards him.

The blue plumed hat, the feathers broken, rolled in the dust behind the man the bullet had hit. Laid on his back, his right arm oddly extended, with a look of shock on his face that was ripped from him as his body registered the pain from his shattered shoulder.

There was no longer any need for stealth.

Standing he stepped towards the edge. The sun was behind him, a bright ball of light shielding him from sight.

One was leaning over his fallen companion, two more had guns in their hands and raised them towards the top of the cliff edge. Nash fired again, this time his bullet killed, tearing into the flesh of the kneeling man just to the left of his spine - it would have carried on tearing his heart apart before exiting and bursting open his rib cage. It was fatal, final and quick and he'd fallen forwards. Dead over his injured companion.

Two shots came his way and Nash retreated from the edge. They might not be able to see him clearly, but that didn't mean they'd not get lucky.

Seven was now five.

Where was shirt tails?

Two were injured or dead, two more were with them, that meant three were somewhere else scaling the heights further along and soon he'd have company on the ridge.

To climb back down, the way he'd come, was too dangerous. There were two braves at the bottom with guns. His guess would be that shirt tails and his two followers would have gone to the east along the ridge where Nantai had been hobbled. From the bottom it looked the more favorable way to make an ascent. So, Nash, the gun slung on his back turned and ran silently along the top of the ridge to the east.

He found what he wanted. A raised rock with sprouting poor sprigs of sagebrush which would provide good cover. Picking up the pace he ran and dropped to the ground behind it, pulling the gun from his back and levelling it back along the ridge in the direction he'd just come. The two colts he pulled from their holsters, he pushed the chambers out, checked them, clicked each one home and laid them next to the Henry. The old one shot he placed to the right, a small stone under the chamber so the grip was raised from the ground. If he needed hold of it in a hurry, he'd not be grabbing a handful of dirt in his fist as well.

# CHAPTER TWELVE

They were faster than he thought and didn't come from the direction he'd anticipated. He twisted where he lay and brought the gun to bear on shirt tails and his companion who were coming head on. The soiled white cotton flapped behind the man as he ran silently in soft moccasins.

Nash had him in his sights of the .44. He pressured the trigger.

Click. Click. Click.

A shout. A warning.

The braves dropped to the ground with the speed of a hawk.

Nash cursed.

Unless he raised himself above the rock, he was behind the man was out of sight.

There was a noise to his right. Taking his eyes off where he knew shirt tails lay, he glanced sideways and saw two more coming towards him from the edge of the ridge.

If he stayed where he was, he'd be overcome by them in a moment.

He didn't hesitate.

Grasping the Henry firmly he rose to his knees, and began to empty the gun. The shots rang out, reverberating from the rocks, high pitched and deafening. The shots stopped their advance. Shirt tails and the brave next to him stayed low and the other two dropped down behind what little cover they could find. The top of a Stetson was just visible, and Nash sent two shots across the top of the ridge aimed towards it.

They hit their mark, parting the hat from its owner, the lead finding a new home inside flesh and bone. The Stetson, freed, rose up in the breeze, and wheeled on its edge away from them.

Five to four.

The Henry had three more shots in her. The tab on the side of the barrel that pressed the rounds down was nearly back to the stock.

He needed there to be only two Indians, or less.

The moment he paused they'd rise towards him.

Two final shots from the Henry towards white tails and his companion and another to the brave on his right.

He didn't pause but with a sadness that hit at his heart he dropped the Henry – useless now – and pulled the colts out with lightning speed.

He placed two shots before both groups, in the dirt, raising a plume of dust from the ridge. It gave him a moment only and in it he threw himself to the left of where he had been, rolling over on the ground to get as far away as he could.

The sand and grit on the ridge were heavy, the winds had carried away the fine dust, and that stirred up by the shots dropped quickly, clearing the brave's view of the ridge.

A moment lapsed.

Nash held his breath.

Three shots landed to his right where he had laid only seconds before.

Nash didn't move.

There were three of them left. Each knew the odds were in their favor, the chances were they'd break cover first to see if they'd made a hit.

Patience.

And he knew the men his faced had as much as he did.

The sun had moved. His hat was no longer covering his neck, and he could feel the hot rays baking the skin on the back of his neck. A fly, drawn by the moisture of his eyes, landed on his lashes. He tried to blink it away, but more than that he couldn't do. To move was to give himself away. He was laid on the ground behind low rocks and he'd not had time to pick a good spot. A sharp rock was digging painfully into his right thigh, but he'd couldn't shift his position to ease the pressure, and through the sleeve on his right arm barbs from a cholla cactus had pierced his skin all the way along his forearm.

There was a sudden scream from below, and the vicious terrible sound of Rock's anger. The dog's terrifying growls and barks as he fought drowned out the man's terrified voice. Nash listened without moving, until there was only one sound rising up from near the homestead – Rock's howl of victory. Whoever they had left below with the horses was no longer his problem.

Four to three.

There was a dead man on the ridge, and the scent of blood had risen on the breeze and circling above them were three ch'ishoogi, turkey vultures. Their keen eyes also on the scene below. When the birds reached the far side of their soaring circle Nash could see them as they glided effortlessly above the ridge. The dark body, white wing edges, and the red turkey-like head that gave the bird its name.

The braves would have seen them as well. Nash allowed himself a slight smile and felt his resolve harden. The cactus hadn't drawn blood yet, but when he moved it would, and he knew the birds would smell it.

Keeping his breathing even, and his eyes on the ridge, Nash waited.

It wasn't the braves who made the first move. It came from a turkey vulture, folding its wings up over, its legs extended it glided across the ridge between Nash and white tails. When it was a dozen feet from the ground it flapped its wings, slowing its speed, before landing with surprising gentleness its wings still wide to stabilize it, beak open, eyes surveying the ridge.

Nash could see all of the bird, and he guessed it was standing on the dead brave. There was no other movement. The vulture stood motionless for a moment, then its head dipped, Nash watched the dark feathers on its back ripple in the breeze. A moment later the vulture raised its head, a long flap of flesh in its beak, with a gulping motion the bloody flesh disappeared, and the bird lowered its head back for another morsel.

Patience.

Just wait.

The second and third turkey vultures ended their glide above the ridge and, taking the same flight path that their leader had, lowered themselves readying for a landing. As the bird's wings widened, readying to slow themselves, close enough for Nash to feel the draught of their passing, he tightened his hold on the guns – ready.

The second bird landed on the ground before the dead man, and the third on top of a man who was not yet ready to be eaten. The brave erupted from where he had lain in a sudden tangle of black feathers.

Nash rose to his knees and fired twice from the colt in his left hand.

Man, and prey fell forward, a black broken wing still raised from the ridge flapping erratically. The other two vultures, abandoning their meal raced forwards taking off in the space between Nash and the other two braves.

The birds for a second obscured their view of Nash, and the shots that came from them went wide. One he heard ping from a rock to his left and another sent an eruption of sand and dust before his right knee.

They were close.

Too close.

Another whir of clicks and the colts replied with four bullets low to the ground, but this time Nash had a mark. And they lifted the man from where he crouched sending him reeling back over, the gun in his right-hand cartwheeling in the air before clattering back amongst the rocks and misfiring.

One.

Above them, the remaining two turkey vultures hovered, the large dark shadows they cast flitting across the ridge.

Nash emptied the colt into the sand in front of white tails, then pulled the one shot from inside his vest and held the Perry ready.

Nash stopped.

Low to the ground, for a moment hidden by the dust that was wheeling in the breeze, he waited.

Nash's eyes were fixed on the clearing dust and sand his bullets had kicked up, looking for the slightest change that would reveal the brave. He nearly missed him. Expecting him to emerge from the middle he was momentarily surprised when the man came from the left of the clearing dust, he'd used it as cover to move away from his dead companion.

In his hand was a revolver – one he'd yet to fire and on his face an expression of malevolent joy.

Nash didn't hesitate.

He didn't wait for the brave to take another step.

The Perry in his right hand spoke with finality. Just once. The bullet landed squarely in the man's chest. For a moment he hung in the air, his arms flung wide by the impact, his own gun slipping from his grip, the shirt flapping around his body before he fell to his knees and then keeled over sideways.

Before he had hit the floor Nash was running. White tails had dropped a Remmington, he lay on his side, he wasn't dead – yet. The bullet had holed his chest to the left of his heart, his hand covered the wound, and blood frothed from his lips. He'd taken a hit to his lungs. It would be slow.

Nash pulled the hunting knife from his belt and severed the brave's throat, giving him an immediate end before picking up the Remmington he'd dropped. Spinning the chamber, he found it held three rounds.

The man next to him was dead, on his back, his mouth open wide, a wide stare looking upwards towards the turkey vultures who would soon be back on the top of the ridge again.

To the right the dead vulture lay dead on top of another brave, the colt's bullets had gone through the bird and taken away the man's lower jaw before exiting from the back of his head. Behind him the ground was splattered with his remains, a large section of the man's brain grey and white, lay in the dust. The texture soft and gelatinous, the color grey and pink surrounded by white fragments of bone and globules of blood. Death for both him and the vulture had been instantaneous.

Nash collected another weapon, tucked it into his belt before he ran, soft footed, to where he'd abandoned the Henry. Retrieving the gun, and making a silent apology to it, he made his way back towards the homestead.

None.

Before Nash started to pull the wooden boards from the cistern, he called out, so the woman knew it was him. She was pale, soaked and the hands he took in his to lift her out trembled.

"They're gone," he reassured smiling.

"Gone?" She repeated.

"In a manner, yes, and we need to be as well," Nash said.

Nantai was tethered with the other horses the braves had brought. The breeze caught in the threads of ginger hair, and they flapped around the saddle bow of one of them, the curved knife in his hand, Nash cut them away.

Lucy, well acquainted with horses, helped, and in a short space of time they were mounted, and between them they led the ownerless buckskins behind them as they headed for Goldsprings. Just after they had set off Rock appeared, padding softly behind them, the fur of his chest and face stained with blood.

Nash shook his head and regarded the dog with a solid blue stare. "And where do you think you've been hiding?"

The dog regarded him for a moment, before taking up a position by the side of Nash's horse. Without looking at the dog, Nash pulled a piece of jerky from his pocket and threw it towards Rock.

# CHAPTER THIRTEEN

They made it to Goldsprings in three days. Given the horses they were leading behind them Nash wanted to stop as little as possible, and the pace was a tough one.

Lucy, exhausted, and falling forwards in her saddle was in danger of sliding from the horse. Nash moved Nantai close, squeezing Lucy's shoulder, he smiled, and brought her horse to a halt next to his.

"This'll make things easier, ma'am," Nash said, wrapping a rope around the woman's waist he fastened it to the saddle horn. "Is that too tight?"

Lucy shook her head.

"Good, it'll stop you falling. I'm sorry ma'am, but I daren't slow the pace, those braves will be missed soon enough, and we'll have more Apache on our tails than I can hold off."

Lucy smiled at him, and before he could reply, kicked her own horse forward again. During the journey Lucy slept fitfully, slumped over in her saddle, the rope taking her weight, then she'd be jolted awake when the buckskin stumbled. But, Nash reasoned, some sleep was better than none. It took three long hard days to reach Goldsprings. It was the end of a journey, something Nash never usually liked, but on this occasion the prospect of a good meal and a solid night's sleep was the reward he wanted the most.

As they neared the town, Nash asked. “You been here before?”

Lucy shook her head. “But Uncle Clem told me that his brother had a town house next to the livery yard and then a ranch out to the west.”

“What’s your uncle’s brother’s names?” Nash asked.

“Nathaniel Waters,” Lucy replied.

Nash nodded.

There were two saloons in Goldsprings, one was the End of the Trail Saloon, he’d been here before, it was a two-bit saloon, and he preferred it over the one-bit Long Way Saloon that served rough whiskey and had rooms to match.

It had been a long while since he had been here, but he remembered it well enough. A wide street, dusty now, the wagon tracks and hoof marks that had once been printed in mud were now baked into the street. There were two saloons and a livery yard part way along on the left.

Nash saw the sign above the entrance to the yard. A little more faded than he remembered and sagging at one end, but it still declared ‘Best Livery in Town.”

A boy, about ten, saw him approach and dropped from his perch on a rail, running barefoot towards him.

“Howdy, sir. McCliff’s is the best livery yard in town, sir. Your horses looks mighty fine, and deserve the best,” the boy declared.

Nash, who had been heading to McCliff’s anyway, decided to play along.

"She's a mighty fine horse, who'd be carin' for her, son?" Nash said, leaning down and patting Nantai's neck.

"Mr McCliffe. It's fifty cents a day for livery or three dollars a week, sir, the best in town, and that includes cleaning your saddle, and if you've clothes need a launderin' then Mrs. McCliffe will take care of that for you," the boy declared, he was walking backwards now in front of Nash. "Just follow me, sir."

Nash hid a smile. There'd be a meal, or a coin, for everyone he brought through the gate to the livery yard. "What about the one further along, I've a memory that was a good yard when I stopped here before."

The boy's eyebrows rose, and he adopted a feigned look of horror. "I couldn't let you take your fine horses there, sir."

"Really? Why?" Nash replied.

The boy shook his head earnestly. "Their feeds full of mold and the water runs through the piss trenches behind the Long Way Saloon before it reaches their yard."

"I'm glad you warned me, son," Nash said, his voice serious.

The boy, a little bolder now, and eager to secure his customer, reached up and wrapped a filthy hand around Nantai's bridle. "Follow me, sir."

"I'm looking for a Nathaniel Water's, you know where his house is, son?" Nash asked.

The boy frowned and pointed across the street. "Right there, sir. The one with the fancy windows."

Nash and Lucy looked where he pointed. The house had a smart wooden front with a half a dozen steps up to a wide veranda at the front. The windows were indeed fancy. The ones on the lower floor were curtained with heavy sashes drawn back with thick gilt loops and upstairs the material was lighter, the tops of the window frames decorated inside with a line of tassels.

Nash smiled, feeling he needed to say something. “It’s a mighty fine house.”

“It sure looks it,” Lucy said, her voice a little nervous.

“Let me see to the horses, and I’ll take you right over,” Nash said.

The boy, hearing the words, grinned delightedly and led them to the yard. As soon as they were through the gates a whiskered man with a grey deformed hat appeared from one of the stalls.

“I’ll take over, Matthew,” then to Nash, “Howdy sir, livery? How long you are looking for?”

Nash dropped easily from the saddle. Until now he’d not even thought about it. Handing the reins to McCliffe he said. “A night at least. I’m fixing to sell those and keep these two.”

McCliffe ran a practiced eye over the buckskins. “Might be that we can cut a deal, son.”

Nash handed the reins to Matthew and said. “I’ll be back soon enough.”

Lucy had already dropped down from the saddle.

"Come on, I'll take you over," Nash said firmly.

Lucy nodded.

The door was answered by a young black girl, her hair neat and topped with a lace cap.

Lucy smiled. "I'm calling on my uncle, Nathaniel Waters, can you let him know Lucy Wright is here."

The girl stared between Lucy and Nash for a moment, her eyes wide, then turned and disappeared without a word along the corridor.

Nash and Lucy looked at each other, bewildered.

A few minutes later an elderly lady, hiding behind the girl appeared, and looked at them from the end of the corridor.

"Ma'am, I'm Lucy Wright, Uncle Clem ...." Lucy swallowed hard, "fell prey to the Indians and, Nash, here has been kind enough to bring me to Goldsprings."

"Lucy?" The woman pushed her way round the black girl. "Nathaniel's niece?"

Lucy smiled. "The very same, ma'am."

"Oh, and Clem and his wife! That's terrible, when did that happen?" The woman said arriving at the doorway.

"About a week back, I guess, ma'am, I've been losing count of the days if the truth be known," Lucy said.

"My poor child, you must come in. Don't stand on the step," The woman waved Lucy forward.

Lucy turned towards Nash. "This is Nash, he saved me from the Indian's and brought me here. I'd have not made it without his help."

Lucy's Aunt looked at Nash dubiously. "Well of course come in as well, I am sure ...."

"Thank you for your hospitality, ma'am, but I've horses to tend to," Nash was already backing down the steps, tipping his hat towards the women.

"Of course, well thank you, Mr Nash for bringing Lucy to me," the woman said, she'd stepped forwards, taken Lucy's arm and was already leading her into the house.

Lucy turned, confusion on her face. "Thank you. I'll see you again before you leave?"

Nash was back in the street. "Yes, ma'am."

The door closed. Nash breathed a sigh of relief and returned to the livery yard.

The boy was watching him return, and McCliffe was still in the yard.

"Is Gilligan's End of The Trail Saloon still the best place to find a bed?" Nash asked McCliffe.

"It is sir. Matthew, come back here and take .... I didn't get your name, sir?" McCliffe replied, not stopping brushing down the horse.

"I didn't give it," Nash replied, then added, "I can find Gilligan's myself, just livery for the night, and take a look at those buckskins and let me know what you think."

McCliffe, not about to lose the chance of a referral continued. "Matthew, go tell Gilligan he's at McCliffe's livery and to make sure he gives him one of the good rooms at the back."

Matthew nodded and darted across the street and was up the three wooden steps and ducked under the batwing doors into Gilligan's Saloon before Nash was half-way across the dusty street. His saddle he'd left at McCliffe's, but his pack was slung over his right shoulder, and the gun case across his back.

The sun was still high in the sky, and the dark interior of the saloon beckoned over the top of the doors. The swinging doors creaked as he set his hands on them, pushing them open, he stepped inside, moving forward into the dim interior and letting them swing back closed behind him, casting a dark shadow over the worn wooden floor. The air was still, dust motes hung suspended in the shafts of light that cut into the interior over the saloon doors. The room was filled with furniture, but as yet, no patrons. It was early in the day. A long, worn bar stretched across one side of the saloon, its surface polished by countless elbows and spilled drinks. The bartender was busy with a cloth, bringing a shine to a line of glasses that sat on the top of the bar. A neat figure, organized, with a clean apron drawn up high on his chest and wrapped around a portly body. He put down the cloth and regarded Nash with an enquiring gaze. Gilligan's was a two-bit saloon.

"What'll it be?"

Nash thought for a moment. He'd been about to ask for beer. Cool, thirst-quenching beer, but the line of small solid glasses on the saloon bar changed his mind.

"Fill me one of them up with whiskey," Nash pointed towards the glasses.

The bartend didn't move. "That'll be two bits, sir."

Nash nodded, fished inside his waistcoat and pulled out one of the silver dollars he'd taken from Kip. "There's pay for the first and for the one after that, and I need a room as well."

The bartender's attitude changed immediately. He swept the coin from the bar, bit it, before stowing it behind the bar. "Four bits for the whiskey, the room'll be a dollar, and if you want a meal then it'll be another fifty cents."

Nash smiled and produced the other two coins that had once belonged to Kip. "Sounds good to me."

The bartender nodded, produced a small clinking pile of change and set it before Nash then he lifted down two bottles from the shelf behind the bar. "You've a choice, son. This 'ere is George Dickel, a Tennessee whiskey. It'll chase the dust from your throat and slide down your throat like warm honey, and this other one is a might fierier, got a kick to her, which would you like?"

Nash smiled. "Honey first and a kick second."

The bartender smiled. "Good choice, son."

Nash watched him draw one of the heavy glasses forward, unstopped the whiskey bottle and filled the glass with a rich golden-brown liquid. When he'd finished he stoppered the bottle and returned it to the shelf.

Nash wrapped his hand around the glass, and turned it in his hand, the amber liquor swirling inside.

"Been a while. No need to rush it, son. It took eight years to make, back in time that was seeds in a field and water in a brook, a lot happens in eight years," the bartender advised, his arm dipped below the counter, and he produced another bottle and carefully poured a measure from it. "My Marthe makes this from apples. I'll join you if I may."

Nash raised the glass in a salute before he set the glass to his lips. Used now to the rough edge of the metal coffee cup or the rim of the water skin the smooth weighty glass felt alien on his lips. Tipping it slowly he allowed a third of the glass to pour into his mouth. His eyes closed his senses delighted in the rounded rich warmth of the whiskey and the deep smoky flavor as it danced on his tongue. The smell from the whiskey glass rose to his nose, rich and smoky, so unlike the last time he had smelt whiskey. Ted's liquor when they'd been on the trail had smelt harsh, alien and even unsettling and out of place on the plains by the campfire. But here, in the saloon, the whiskey was at home. The aroma mixing with the smell of aged wood, tobacco smoke, spilt spirits, polish, cooking aromas and the dusty interior of the saloon.

With a satisfied nod, Nash set the empty glass down and looked back at the bartender. The glint in his eyes revealed his desire for another round. Recognizing the cowboy's appreciation for the drink, the bartender nodded, understanding the unspoken request. “And now this will chase that honey all the way to your stomach.”

The bartender had unstopped the second bottle. He selected a clean glass, filled it and slid it towards Nash, before placing the whiskey bottle back on the shelf.

Once again Nash lifted it to his lips. The second glass of whiskey brought with it an even deeper sense of contentment, it was hotter, and as the bartender had said chased the first drink to his stomach warming his innards. It had spice to it as well that left his mouth warm even after he'd swallowed the whiskey.

Nash emptied the glass, his eyes lingering on the empty interior for a moment sadly before placing it down solidly on the bar.

“Another?” the bartend asked, smiling.

The bottle, half full, sat on the shelf. Nash pointed at it. “How much?”

“Good choice, son. Those coins you got there will cover it,” the bartender said.

Nash slid the coins towards him and took the bottle and pocketed a glass.

Soon Nash was shown into one of the good rooms at the back. “No noise from the street, and not over the saloon neither,” Marthe, the bartender's wife had said as she unlocked the door.

Nash had a key pressed into his hand and was alone in the simple room. A bed, a wooden stand with a porcelain ewer on top, and a window, shuttered and looking over the plains away from the town. The floor was bare boards, swept clean and a posy of dried flowers in a bottle sat on top of a slightly ragged lace doilie in an attempt to decorate the room.

Nash pressed a hand to the bed, the covers were clean, the bed soft. He deposited his dusty hat on the bed post and sat on the edge of the bed and pulled his boots from his feet before stretching out on the bed.

The whiskey had done its work. Numbing his senses and within a few minutes after his eyes had closed, he was asleep.

When he awoke there was no longer any light coming through the shutter slats and the room was in a rich darkness. What had woken him was a tap at the door.

"Mr Sir," it was the boy, Matthew, tapping on his door.

From somewhere he couldn't quite explain came a sudden acute bolt of disappointment.

"What is it, son?" Nash called from the bed.

"Best steak in the county, sir, and cooked up with beans," Mrs. Martha would like to know if you'd like a plate filled?" the boy called through the closed door.

If the whiskey had sated his thirst, it also lit his hunger and at the word steak there was the unmistakable rumble of hungry complaint from his guts.

"Tell Mrs. Martha, I'll be right down," Nash replied swinging his legs from the bed.

"And the steak?" Matthew said, not wanting to leave before he'd secured an order.

"And steak and beans," Nash confirmed as he began to draw his boots on.

When he walked down the creaking stairs back to the saloon, he found the atmosphere was lively, with the clinking of glasses and the occasional burst of laughter echoing through the air. Cowboys, adorned in their weathered hats and dusty boots, gathered around wooden tables, engaging in games of poker and exchanging tales of their adventures under the watchful eye of the saloon's bartender.

The saloon's soundtrack was now a symphony of clinking poker chips, the soft strumming of a guitar, and the occasional outburst of rowdy laughter or heated disputes.

Before he'd reached the bottom of the steps the bartender appeared. "I've saved a table for you, here. Beer or whiskey?"

"Whiskey," Nash confirmed seating himself in the creaking chair.

The steak was thick, well cooked and dripping with gravy, and the rest of the plate was well filled with a bean stew and a plate was set next to him with fresh baked bread. It was, after weeks of trail food, a feast for a king. The rich aromas and tasteful fare absorbing his attention. There was a poker game taking place a few tables away, and the players commentary provided the entertainment as he ate. It was tempting to join them, but he knew his mind was too tired for cards, the whiskey and good food was making him think of the bed upstairs.

Nash finished his meal, and pushed the plate away from him, drawing the whiskey glass closer.

Where to go next?

Maybe he could find another man like McKiddery, but better. He'd liked the man, he was charismatic, and didn't care that Red was a half-breed, some men did, McKiddery said it made him a better man to live on the plains, a better hunter and tracker, and Red had liked that.

McKiddery went too far when he tried to take over the town of Dawn Springs and his short tenure had come to an end when a group of more loyal Texas Rangers arrived and there'd been a show down that had left McKiddery flat on his back in the dust of the street with a dozen bullet holes in his chest.

It had started to go wrong a long time ago he guessed. There'd been signs, plenty of them along the way, but he knew he'd chosen not to heed them. McKiddery had let greed sneak beneath his skin, he'd rewarded those around him, even Red, and he'd argue that his way was the only way. And when you had a warm whiskey in your hand, listening to a man who you had respect for, it was hard to see that he was wrong. It was much easier to let the liquor roll sweetly down your throat, push the dollars inside your jacket and smile.

Until it was too late.

The rogue ranger had been abandoned by his gang in the end and Red high-tailed it out of Dawn Springs on his own and he had found his way to the dusty town of Green Hollow.

The memory of his final day there wasn't a welcome one. Nash threw the last of the whiskey down his throat and headed for his room.

The following day. Well slept and well fed he concluded the deal with McCliffe. He didn't get as much as the horses were worth, but on account of how he'd come by them it was a good deal. When he'd left Oatman he'd only had a few dollars to his name, delivering the letter to Vardy's pard was supposedly where his next few would come from – but that had never happened. He sold five of the six buckskins, they should have fetched him $25 a piece but they'd settled on $50 for them all and free livery for Nantai and the remaining buckskin while he was in town.

Kip's pockets had provided three silver dollars, good coinage and worth more than their face value. They had paid for his room and board, so he had enough to keep him going for a while until he found work somewhere else. If he wanted to.

# CHAPTER FOURTEEN

The wooden floorboards creaked softly under Lucy's boots as she climbed the narrow staircase of the saloon. The air was thick with the scent of whiskey and tobacco, but her heart raced for a different reason. She reached the door to Nash's room, a simple wooden barrier. She knocked, and heard his voice from the other side.

With a gentle push, she entered, the dim light spilling in from the window illuminating Nash, who was leaning against A worn dresser, his hat tilted low over his brow. He looked up, surprise flashing in his deep-blue eyes, and for a moment, the world outside faded away.

"I hope you don't mind me callin' on you, sir?" Lucy said, from where she stood in the doorway to Nash's room, her cheeks suddenly flushed.

Nash smiled. "Not at all, come on in. It's a pleasure ma'am. How did it go with your Uncle Clem's brother?"

Lucy's face saddened as she closed the door.

"Not good, huh!" Nash said.

Lucy shook her head. "Uncle Clems brother, passed away last fall, and his wife's been struggling since. Seemed he owed the bank money and they lost the ranch, and she is set to lose the house as well. It might look grand on the outside sir, but she's sold nearly every piece of furniture. She already looks after Alice, the negro girl we saw, she's dumb, and her husband owed a debt of gratitude."

"So another mouth to feed wasn't welcome," Nash concluded for her. "Don't feel bad. Times are hard for some folks right now."

"I don't blame her, she's so ashamed she can't help me, but the poor woman has nothing left," Lucy said, flinging her arms wide.

Nash let out a long breath. The world sometimes just wasn't fair, and something inside him told him that things needed evening up.

"I've not told you all the truth. There didn't seem any need to, and I didn't want to worry you none. Ted was going to Bakersfield to register his claim, that's true enough, and another mine owner by the name of Vardy, sent one of his men to kill Ted out on the plains. No doubt so he could take Ted's claim," Nash paused, watching her closely to see how she would react.

Lucy's eyes were wide. "That's terrible. What happened?"

"Well, let's just say the man Vardy sent won't be causing anyone any trouble again," Nash grinned.

Lucy nodded her understanding.

"I was taking him West so he could find a legal man to help get his claim back, but I got my doubts about that working. Men like Vardy ain't going to take notice of a piece of paper, the only law they respect is hot lead," Nash said folding his arms and leaning back against the dresser.

"What are you saying?" Lucy said slowly.

Nash smiled. "I could claim I made it to Bakersfield, where I met with Ted Murphy's widow. Now the law says if a man dies then his claim goes to his wife."

"Who's going to believe that?" Lucy said aghast. "You said Ted came from Ireland alone."

"Anyone I point these at, I would imagine," Nash said, in each hand with a speed that left her speechless a gun had appeared. "I used to go by a different name, ma'am, until I found I needed some peace in my life."

Lucy looked from the guns to his face. "What name was that?"

"Red Cartwright," Nash said.

Lucy's eyes widened and she pointed towards him. "You're Red Cartwright?"

"Yes, ma'am," Nash said, smoothly holstering the guns. "I hope I'm not making you nervous now you know who I am?"

Lucy shook her head. "You've been nothing but a fine gentleman since the moment I met you."

"I need to tell you something else as well," Nash said. "Ted, he misfired his gun, didn't get it clear of the holster and ... well .... he was bleeding bad and I didn't want to leave him to the Indians, so that last shot you heard, well that was from me, ending his suffering. I couldn't have saved him, ma'am, but I want you to know that's what I did."

Lucy's face was grim as she took in what he was telling her. "I thank you for your honesty, sir."

"Many wouldn't," Nash said bluntly.

"This mine owner, Vardy you called him, he doesn't know who you are?" Lucy asked.

Nash shook his head. "No, if he did he wouldn't have sent one of his men out on his own to kill Ted."

"So how come you were working for him?" Lucy asked, confusion in her voice.

"I was part of McKiddery's outfit, you might have heard of them, down near Dawn Springs?" Nash explained, he'd removed his hat and put it next to the ewer.

"Sure, everyone's heard of McKiddery," Lucy replied.

"Well, I was with him. Some liked him, some didn't. Kinda depended on who you were," Nash said thoughtfully.

"Uncle Clem thought we needed more like him, to stand up for men when the law wasn't right," Lucy said, nodding.

"It wasn't always like that, ma'am. McKiddery always had a newspaper man with him, what he wrote wasn't always quite what happened," Nash replied slowly.

"I heard he was shot in Dawn Springs, set upon by some rangers who'd been in the pay of a ranch owner to get rid of McKiddery," Lucy said.

Nash looked at her. "And what else did you hear?"

"There was a shoot-out in Dawn Springs, and he took out a dozen of them before they got him," Lucy continued.

Nash smiled.

"What?" Lucy said.

"Well, it seems his newspaper fella was still writing stories," Nash fished inside his jacket and pulled out a worn black and white photograph. "I don't know why I keep it."

It was a photograph of McKiddery. He had been put in a coffin and the coffin propped against the wall of the sheriff's office, a warning to all. His eyes were open, his clothes crumpled, and even in death he was shackled at the wrists.

Lucy took the photograph from him. "Why did they tie his hands after they shot him?"

"I think it's something they do so you know the picture is of a man on the wrong side of the law," Nash accepted the picture back, he glanced again at Mckiddery before sliding the picture away inside a pocket out of sight again.

"Maybe you keep it because you don't want to end up like him," Lucy suddenly suggested.

Nash started, and looked at her smiling, then he said thoughtfully, "You know, ma'am, you might be right. I don't want to end up like him, in more ways than one."

"Then what happened? I heard ...." Lucy's voice trailed off.

Nash smiled. "You heard Red Cartwright killed the sheriff in Green Hollow. That I drew on him first, fired the only shot and killed him while he was sat in the saloon in cold blood."

Lucy blushed. "Well, yes."

"It's sort of true. The part about me killing the sheriff sure is, but that damned fool pulled his gun first, and, after riding with Mckiddery for so long I just got in before he did. Or so I thought," Nash said.

"But you said he fired first?" Lucy said, confusion creasing her brow.

"Well, some don't see it like that. The sheriff he was full of whiskey, and the shot he did get off went through the wood of the bar, nowhere near me," Nash replied. "He was drunk, fired through his holster, so when he was laid on the floor it looked like he'd never drawn a gun."

"In my experience, whiskey makes men meaner than normal," Lucy replied, folding her arms.

"After that I decided, I didn't want to work with a gun anymore," Nash said, then added grinning, "And there was a price on a wanted poster with my name on it."

"What did you do?" Lucy asked.

"I just headed out, took Nantai, ended up in Oatman, and started to work for Vardy almost a year ago. I keep an old beaten-up Perry in my holster, dressed like you see me now, and no-one ever gives me a second look. Kept me on the trail where I like to be and that's enough, I've no grand ambitions like some men," Nash said simply.

"So, you are suggesting that we go back and claim Ted's mining rights?" Lucy asked slowly.

"I am," Nash replied bluntly.

"How?" Lucy said.

Nash grinned, the guns in his hands again, the draw so quick she'd missed it. "We just need to plan this right."

There were tears in Lucy's eyes.

Nash dropped the guns back into the holsters and crossed the room towards her. He wrapped his arms around her and pulled her close. Laying his head on top of hers he said. "Ma'am, I'll not let you down."

"Please, stop calling me ma'am," Lucy said quietly, her arms sliding around him. Drawing him closer.

"Lucy," he murmured, a hint of a smile breaking the rugged lines of his face. The flickering candlelight danced across his chiseled features and rippled in her long soft brown hair.

"That's the first time you've used my name," Lucy said raising her face from his chest to meet his eyes.

Nash's expression was serious, his rough hand caressed her cheek. "Do you want it to be the last?"

Lucy shook her head. "No, I don't, even though I think your trouble, Red Cartwright," she said, trying to maintain her composure, but her voice trembled with excitement.

"Only the good kind," he said, his gaze locking onto hers, intense and unwavering.

In that moment, the room seemed to pulse with unspoken desires. Lucy's breath hitched as Nash leaned closer, his warm breath mingling with hers. The world outside faded into a blur, and all that mattered was the heat radiating between them. The air in Nash's room was thick with anticipation, a palpable energy that crackled like static.

"Come here," he said softly, his voice a low rumble that sent shivers down her spine. He lowered his head towards hers, his eyes dark and inviting, and Lucy felt herself moving toward him, as if pulled by an unseen thread.

"Lucy," he murmured, his breath brushing against her cheek, sending a thrill through her. "I've wanted to do this since the moment I laid eyes on you."

She felt a rush of heat flood her cheeks, and before she could respond, Nash cupped her face in his rough hands, his touch gentle yet firm. He leaned in, their lips just a breath away. The moment stretched, filled with unspoken words and longing, as if the universe itself were holding its breath. Then, as if the world had finally given its blessing, their lips met—softly at first, a tentative exploration that quickly ignited into something fierce and passionate. Lucy melted against him, her hands finding their way to his shoulders, feeling the strength in his muscles beneath the fabric of his shirt.

Nash deepened the kiss, pulling her closer, their bodies fitting together like pieces of a puzzle. Every worry, every doubt faded away as they lost themselves in each other. The kiss was a perfect blend of sweetness and heat, a promise of what was to come.

When they finally pulled apart, Lucy's breath came in short gasps, her eyes sparkling with a mix of surprise and exhilaration. Nash rested his forehead against hers, a satisfied smile playing on his lips.

"Now that's a kiss I won't forget," he said, his voice thick with emotion.

"Neither will I," Lucy replied, her heart soaring as she gazed into his eyes, knowing that this was just the beginning.

Nash lifted her easily in his arms and stepped across the room towards the bed, a simple wooden frame draped in rough linens, but it held a promise of something more intimate tonight. Nash gazed into her eyes with a mixture of admiration and hunger.

They awoke early, the sun sending bright morning rays into the room. Lucy lay close to Nash, her arm across his chest and her head resting on his shoulder.

"So is your name Red or Nash?" Lucy asked.

"Red was just what McKiddery called me. My mother called me Na'ashjii, little storm," Nash shrugged. "It's hard to say, and my grandmother just called me Nash. Apache don't go in for names like folks like you do."

"So why did Mckiddery call you Red Cartwright?" Lucy said confused.

Nash smiled. "Pretty simple. My father's name was Thomas Cartwright and, but the newspaper man McKiddery had with him was called Nash, so they took to calling me Red on account of my Apache blood."

"But now you use Nash?" Lucy said.

Nash grinned. "Don't blame me, ma'am, those wanted posters say Red Cartwright and I've no mind to get my neck stretched on account of something that wasn't my fault."

"Tell me about McKiddery," Lucy said.

"McKiddery was ..." Nash closed his eyes. "I guess like a father, or so I thought. Treated me well, taught me plenty, and had time for me. I liked the man. Hell, everyone in his company liked him."

"Something must have gone wrong, though, if you left him in Dawn Springs?" Lucy asked after a moment.

Nash sat back, his eyes fastened on the horizon, his expression suddenly dark. "It did, and I closed my eyes to it, for a long time. I could speak Apache, negotiate with them on McKiddery's behalf, he persuaded me I was keeping the peace. Allowing them and the settlers to live alongside each other, but that weren't the truth of the matter. Apache had no choice but to do what they did, they were fighting for their way of life, one McKiddery didn't want to understand. He'd pay off the elders to take their followers to the reservations, but that's not the Apache way."

Nash's gaze was fixed on the rough ceiling above them. "I'd got myself in the middle, don't rightly know how. But I was a traitor to both sides. I'd helped chase the Apache out of their territory and then I left Mckiddery to face his end on his own."

"But you'd found out what Mckiddery was like, so no one could blame you for that, surely?" Lucy said,

Nash turned and looked at her straight in the face, their eyes met, and he said truthfully. "I'm half white and half Apache, and it seems I've ended up in the middle of that trouble, and I can see both sides, I truly can, ma'am. And worse, I can see there's no answer. I've been a traitor to both sides, so now I just prefer my own company on the plains."

Lucy didn't answer straight away, wrapping her arm tighter around him she pulled herself closer. "Where we end up isn't always where we want to be."

Nash pulled her closer, kissing the top of her head. "Let's move on to Oatman and see if we can't even things up a little. After I sold the horses, I've enough dollars for what we need to buy."

"What do we need?" Lucy was confused.

"For a start. If you'll beg my pardon, ma'am, Ted Murphy's widow isn't arriving in Oatman looking like you do now," Nash said, grinning and hoping his words wouldn't offend.

Lucy looked across the room at the worn shirt and pants that lay across the back of a chair. "I think I see what you mean."

"We'll fix you up with some ladies clothes before we leave and I'll need some rounds as well, and provisions," Nate said.

Goldsprings provided everything they needed. They shared one more night in the saloon and the following day set out back towards Oatman. Rock trailing behind them.

# CHAPTER FIFTEEN

Mr Vardy's office was different. Kip was no longer propping up the wall next to the door, instead there was a man there Nash didn't recognize. Another Mexican, a lot shorter than Kip, and his face didn't hold the same malevolence as Kip's had.

"Come to see Mr Vardy, can you tell him Nash is here," Nash said, he'd taken his hat from his head and was holding it in both hands close to his chest, his hands rolling the brim nervously.

The Mexican pushed himself away from the wall slowly, his eyes running up and down Nash, and he pushed the door open and disappeared inside, he emerged a moment later.

"Put yer pieces on the rail out here," he said as he stepped back into the light.

Nash, now wearing a Mexican blanket poncho, hitched it back over one shoulder and unbuckled the gun belt with the old Perry and lay it over the rail.

"Much obliged," Nash said, his tone friendly.

The Mexican didn't say anything but just scowled at him and nodded towards the door.

Stepping inside Nash was transported back in time. Nothing had changed, the cigar smoke was still rising from the sides of Vardy's hat, the polished intricate mahogany box was still in the same place on the desk.

Only Vardy had changed. Last time he'd come into the office he'd had to wait while Vardy finished up what he was doing, and that was generally the case. Vardy liked to keep men waiting, Nash guessed it help boost the fat man's feeling of self-importance. Whatever it was, he had abandoned the practice today and his eyes met Nash's as soon as he stepped into the office.

"Son, you're back sooner than I would have expected?" Vardy said, a frown creasing the fat on his forehead.

"We had trouble on the trail, Mr Vardy. I'm afraid to tell you Ted Murphy died; we were set upon a day into the ride. Ted took a shot in his guts, I got him away, but he didn't make it to Bakersfield, sir," Nash said sadly, his hat respectfully clasped in both hands before him.

"That is bad news," Mr Vardy said, his piglike eyes still fastened on Nash, "Who attacked you?"

"It was at night, didn't get a good look. May have been one or two, I can't rightly say. Ted plugged one of them, I heard him screaming as I helped him get on his horse, and we hightailed it out of there," Nash explained.

Mr Vardy nodded. "And Mr Murphy?"

Nash shook his head, a grim expression on his face. "It was a gut shot, no saving him. I did what I could, he made me promise to find his wife and bring her back here to take on his claim. Said she'd pay me well enough to get her here and so I brung her back with me. I have some more bad news; in the confusion I lost my pack when we were attacked and the letter for your pard was in it."

"His wife?" Vardy said, his voice incredulous, a fat finger prodded the brim of his hat and tipped it backwards on his head.

"Yes sir, Lucy Murphy," Nash replied. "And I brung her, just like Ted asked me to. Said you'd help her with the claim and such. Not something I knows much about, and I'm sorry Mr Vardy about the letter."

"Yes, no doubt. Where is she?" Vardy said.

"She's down at Dante's Saloon, they have a room for her, and I said I'd come and see you first. Explain what had happened, poor woman is still mighty upset over her husband's death," Nash said, his voice a little halting, he was always happy to play the fool for Vardy, it worked in his favor. "Do you have any other work for me, Mr Vardy?"

Vardy looked at him blankly for a moment, before he shook his head waving his hand towards the door. "No need of you right now, son."

Nash nodded his head. "Thank you Mr Vardy, and I'm mighty sorry about your letter."

"I am sure you are, go on," Vardy waved his hand towards the door.

Nash emerged, fitted his hat back on his head and retrieved his gun belt, fastening it back on with ease, settling it on his hips. He tipped his hat towards the Mexican who just scowled at him again and dropped down the creaking wooden boards towards the dusty street. As he walked away a pleased expression played on his face. The meeting had gone well, very well.

Dante's saloon was the better of the two that Oatman possessed, on the opposite side of the wide street was Monty's Saloon, and it was to this one Nash went. It was rough in all respects, the furniture, the bar and the clientele. It served cheap liquor in chipped glasses and a standard meal, a bean and meat stew, served from a cooking pot at the back of the saloon.

Nash didn't want a drink, but he did want to sit at the table out front and that meant buying whiskey and stew. He also wanted to be left alone, so he ordered a drink and a bowl of stew, paid and took them outside and settled himself down to watch Dante's saloon opposite.

The stew wasn't bad, it was hot and filling and came with a lump of bread. It catered to the miners and prospectors' hunger. After a long day's toil, they wanted their belly's filling and a few glasses of whiskey to wash it down with, before they finally slept.

Nash didn't have long to wait.

Vardy, accompanied by half a dozen of his boys arrived at Dante's saloon. Nash had no fear that there'd be any sort of trouble. He'd picked a time of day when the saloon would be full, so there'd be plenty there to witness his meeting with Lucy, and they'd arranged for her to be in the saloon taking a meal, so the meeting had to take place in public.

And it seemed to have been a short meeting. Vardy stomped down the wooden steps of Dante's saloon back into the street only a few minutes later, a scowl on his face. Nash, in no haste to leave, finished his meal and gulped down the whiskey before rising and making his way along the street away from the saloons. There were some scraps left from his meal and he pocketed them and then turned left just after the bathhouse and walked back towards the rear of Dante's. The main entrance was at the front, but the saloon offered livery as well and so there were steps up at the back of the saloon for those who'd got horses in the stables behind it. At the back, tied up, the broken ear hanging mutinously over one eye, was Rock.

"Not long now," Nash said, handing over the food he'd brought, ruffling the fur on the dog's ears. "Just not going to be safe tonight, and I know what a nose you have for trouble."

Nash headed up the stairs. Lucy was still in the saloon, but she'd been watching for him, and when she saw him taking the stairs she abandoned her meal and followed him.

Neither spoke until Lucy had closed the door to the rented room.

"What did he say?" Nash asked.

"Offered me his condolences and asked me to come to his house this evening and share a meal with him, and he'd gladly help me out," Lucy said, then added. "That was it."

Nash nodded. "And you said you would?"

"I did, like we agreed," Lucy said.

"He was going to invite you to his house or his office, somewhere private, had to be one or the other, his house is out of the way," Nash said.

"What do you think he'll do?"

"Scare you off, or worse," Nash said bluntly. "I can take care of his boys, are you sure you can do this? Now the time is here, I don't like putting you anywhere near Vardy."

Lucy smiled. "I'll be fine."

"Just keep him talking," Nash said, no longer sure about the plan. "We'll go to the mine office and the sheriffs on our way there, didn't want to before you met with him because you can be sure Vardy will get to hear about it straight away if we were asking about Ted's claim."

"So, we go now?" Lucy asked.

"We do, then I'll take you to his house," Nash said, then a smile flickered across his lips. Dressed now in women's clothes, tightly fitting at her waist, and declaring the shape of her body, she looked even more beautiful. "But we don't need to go anywhere for a while yet."

Their eyes locked for a moment, a silent promise passing between them. Then, with a sudden surge of emotion, Nash leaned in, capturing her lips with his own. The kiss ignites with a fiery passion. Lucy's fingers weave through his tousled hair, feeling the strength of his presence, while he deepens the kiss, tilting his head to explore the sweetness of her lips.

The mine office was on the main street a dozen or so buildings along from Vardy's. They made their approach directly down the street, Nash had no doubt that Vardy's men would have seen them and reported it to their boss.

The mine office was small, no longer big enough to serve the needs of the prospecting and mining town Oatman had become. On the rear wall was a large map of the area, and marked upon it were the names of the claims, and next to each a number. There were shelves on the right side of the wall holding wooden boxes, each of them penned with a letter, A to Z, and holding the details of those who had claims in the area. There were several boxes for popular letters like M, P, T and S, and X,Y and Z shared one box together.

The rest of the room was given over to a small desk behind which a small man sat, his shirt sleeves held away from his wrists with cuff garters, to stop the ink catching on them, his hat hung on a peg on the wall, the bridge of his nose housed a pair of round rimmed spectacles and his head was topped with thinning sandy hair. When they came into the office, he paused, the pen still in his hand and gazed at them over the top of his spectacles, a questioning look on his face.

It was Lucy who spoke, stepping forwards towards the clerk, a smile on her face. “Sir, I hope you can be of help. My husband was Mr Murphy, he had a claim hereabouts, and unfortunately ....” Lucy paused for a theatrical sniff, raising a handkerchief to her eyes, “he has passed away, and I need to get his claim transferred to myself.”

“Mr Murphy? Ted Murphy?” the clerk said, laying down his pen and rising.

“Yes sir. He was my husband,” Lucy said, still dabbing her eyes.

The clerk extended a hand towards her, and she took it. “I am sorry to hear about your husband, ma’am. I can check our records, but I have a good memory and I’m not so sure we have a claim in that name.”

Lucy looked concerned. “I am sure you do. He told me about it in his letters. And it’s all I have; I’m intending to transfer it into my name and then sell it.”

“Well, I’ll check for you,” the clerk said. He rounded the desk and took down a box with the letter M on the front, adjusting his glasses, he began to shuffle through the papers in the box slowly.

Lucy and Nash watched him. He got to the end and began to shake his head. “I thought I was right, there’s nothing in here belonging to a Murphy.”

“Maybe, it’s in the other box,” Nash pointed towards a second box on the shelf marked with the letter M.

The clerk turned a sour look on Nash. “If it was going to be here it would be in this box, son.”

"Why don't you just check, in case," Nash said, his tone conversational.

"I don't know who you think you are, son ...." The clerk stopped mid-sentence, and his expression froze. Nash, smiling, had a gun in his hand and it was pointing directly at the man's chest.

"Alright, I'll check," the clerk said quickly, his voice high pitched with nerves, his eyes on the colt.

"Why don't you slowly lift that box down and then sit yourself in that there chair while Mrs. Murphy has a look through the box," Nash suggested, his voice pleasant.

"I'm happy to look," the clerk protested weakly.

"Well, I'm not. Just set the box on the desk and then sit yourself down," Nash instructed.

Realizing he had no choice the clerk complied. Placing the second box marked 'M' in front of Lucy and then stepping back.

"Now sit down in that chair nice and slowly, and put your hands on the chair arms where I can see them," Nash said motioning towards the chair with the gun barrel.

Lucy had already pulled the box towards her and was flipping through the contents. The clerk licked his lips and switched his gaze nervously between Lucy and Nash.

"Here it is," Lucy announced triumphantly, holding a folded sheet in the air. "Mr Edward Murphy."

"Well now, ain't that a surprise?" Nash said to the clerk.

"Sure is," the clerk replied weakly.

"Now we found it you can assign this to Murphy's wife, isn't that right?" Nash asked.

"I can, but .... But rightly I should see a marriage certificate ...." the clerk replied.

"I've got that right here," Nash said, from the second holster he drew another colt, spun it in the air for a moment and brought the barrel round to point directly at the clerk. "Does that look like a marriage certificate to you?"

Ther clerk swallowed hard.

"Well?" Nash asked again.

"It sure does, sir," the clerk said.

"Good, hand him that sheet and let's get this claim in your name," Nash said to Lucy.

Lucy put the sheet on the desk and slid it across towards the clerk.

The clerk pulled his chair closer to the desk, settled his glasses on his nose and picked up the pen he had abandoned when the pair had entered his office. "I can assign it here, Mrs. Murphy can sign here and you, sir, can be the witness. What name shall I put down for you?"

"Red Cartwright," Nash replied.

The clerk looked up quickly, his eyes moving from the guns to Nash's face.

"You heard right," Nash said.

"Yes, sir," the clerk returned his attention to the paper and for the next few moments the only noise in the room was the scratching of his pen on the paper. "There we go, if you sign here, Mrs. Murphy."

Lucy took the pen and signed next to where the Clerk had penned Mrs. Murphy. Nash took the pen in his left hand and waved the clerk back away from the desk with the barrel. "Go on, move back."

"I didn't know you were left-handed?" Lucy said.

Nash, his eyes never leaving the clerk, replied. "I'm not, ma'am, makes no difference to me which I use."

Nash dipped the pen, and signed next to his name, his eyes never leaving the clerk. "Now we just need to know where it is. There's a number ma'am on the top corner, and I'm guessing it'll match up with a number on that wall over there. Am I right?"

"Yes, sir," the clerk nodded.

Lucy lifted the page. "One, seven, three, four."

"One, seven, three, four. You go point it out for Mrs. Murphy," Nash said to the clerk.

The clerk glanced nervously over his shoulder at the map.

"Go on. I've a notion that you know exactly where it is," Nash said, moving a little closer to the desk.

"Well, it's around here somewhere," the clerks shaking hand hovered near the top right-hand side of the map.

"Find it," Nash commanded his voice cold.

The clerk's finger tapped the map. "Here it is."

"Turn that chair towards the wall in that corner, and have a sit down," Nash said, waving the gun in the direction he wanted the clerk to go.

When the clerk was seated, he moved to examine the map. Next to the claim number the name Murphy had been struck through and another added underneath. Vardy.

Confirmation of everything Nash had suspected, and the clerk had been complicit.

"You knew Vardy took another man's claim?" Nash growled over the clerk's shoulder where he sat shaking in the chair.

"I didn't have no choice. What can I do against Mr Vardy?" The clerk's voice was high pitched and filled with nerves.

Nash didn't reply. He knew what type of man Vardy was, he was a bossman with a dozen armed men around him to enforce his rule. He had money, and money bought muscle. That made his word the law.

"I'm going to see Mr Vardy shortly, so I need you to stop right where you are. Now I'm sure you're a trustworthy soul, and I'm sure you'd not go telling on what just happened in here. But I'm just suspicious of men to the core, so, I'll just make sure you stop here in my own way," Nash had a coil of rope around his shoulder and he unhooked it, the clerk realizing what was about to happen rolled his eyes, but made no further complaint as he was bound and gagged in his chair – after all it was a better outcome than the alternative that Nash's gun had recently offered him.

Nash locked the mine office door from the inside, pocketed the key and they left via a window at the back. Nash was sure the clerk would be discovered eventually, but hopefully that would be after they had paid Vardy a visit.

The next stop would be the sheriff's office on the way to Vardy's. That was a visit Nash was going to me on his own.

# CHAPTER SIXTEEN

Mrs. Murphy, trailed by Nash, his hat pulled low and casting his eyes about him nervously, the blanket hanging raggedly down to his knees, arrived at Vardy's house.

It was at the edge of the town, a wide wooden house, surrounded by a fence, there were ten steps up to the veranda that ran around the front of the house and idling on there were two of Vardy's men. The Mexican he had seen earlier that day at Nash's office and another man he didn't recognize. Both were there to ensure Vardy's security.

"What you brought that damn fool with you for?" Vardy said as he appeared at the front door, pointing at Nash.

Lucy turned but before she could say anything Nash replied. "Sorry, Mr Vardy."

"You will be. Clear off," Vardy said, then to Lucy, "Beware his type, ma'am, he's nothing more in his mind than seeing how many dollars he can get from you. Them half-cur Indians are all the same."

Lucy, her mouth open, was unsure what to say, but managed. "I'm sure you're right, Mr Vardy."

Vardy smiled at that. "I sure am. Them half-breeds are outcast by both sides, no-one wants them, the breeding ain't right."

"Breeding?" Lucy queried.

Vardy nodded. "A white man's seed don't work well with Indian blood. Look at Nash, he's a fool. It wasn't meant to be mixed. It ain't Christian." He concluded with a grim look on his face.

Lucy put her hand to her mouth, and managing to sound horrified said, “I didn’t realize he was half Indian.”

Vardy tapped his nose. “He tries to hide it, but it’s there alright. You want to keep away from him, ma’am, his type can’t be trusted.”

“Oh my,” Lucy gasped. “It sounds like I have had a lucky escape.”

Vardy took her arm, and Lucy let him. Nash had told her to smile and entertain Vardy, that’s all she had to do. Pretend to enjoy his company over a meal. How hard could that be?

"I'm sorry, ma'am, I've shocked you. I forget this is no place for a fine city woman like yourself. Please forgive me," Vardy said as he led her indoors.

"Of course, it's all been a very difficult time for me," Lucy said, smiling weakly.

"Of course, losing your husband so unexpectedly can't have been easy. Come on inside," Vardy invited. "I don't often get the opportunity of good company."

The room he showed Lucy into stopped her in her tracks for a moment. A parlor, neat, tidy and beautifully decorated. On the mantle two white porcelain dogs watched her enter, the floor was covered with a thick deep-red patterned rug, the table covered in a delicate cloth. On top of it crystal glasses, shining cutlery, plates and lit candles that wafted in the draught from the open door.

Vardy smiled. "My mother's room, the Lord rest her soul. Brought all this with her from London England when my father brought her here. I don't use it often, but I like to keep it how she would have wanted it."

"It's beautiful," Lucy said, her words honestly spoken.

Vardy removed his hat, hung it on a peg on the back of the door and turned back. That's when she was stricken with the full horror of the man. The wide brim hid his head, and shaded his face, the constant plume of cigar smoke also served to veil his appearance.

Now that the full light of the room fell on him, she could see the limp greasy thinning strands of hair that clung to his round, moonlike head. Where the hat brim had sat there was a dark and ugly band of filth and moist sweat. His eyes, recessed in the fat of his face, were like those of a pig, small, beady and fastened upon her with undisguised lust. As she watched his tongue flicked out and licked his lips, revealing a row of uneven yellow and black teeth.

Lucy swallowed and turned her attention back to the table. "Your mother sure had mighty fine taste."

"Sit, please," Vardy waved a hand towards one of the two chairs drawn up to the table. Lucy lowered herself reluctantly into one and Vardy, now behind her, helped to push the chair forward. His breath warm, fetid and stinking plumed around her as he breathed out.

Vardy rounded the table and sat opposite her. "Now, ma'am, I've a meal to offer you and I hope you are going to enjoy it."

A moment later the door opened and a silver tray born by a negro entered with their first course.

Meanwhile Outside.

Nash hunched over, and shambling had made his way from the house, or so any casual observer might have thought. The Mexican blanket, a dirty cream with a simple geometric pattern he pulled from his head, reversed it and

put it back on. The inside was the color of night, and Nash darted left and disappeared behind the big barn that stood to the left of Vardy's house. Vardy's boys lived in the ranch house next to the barn, and he could hear their voices through the thin wooden walls. Nash, his back to the wall, closed his eyes for a moment and focused on the sounds inside.

They were playing cards, and drinking.

Patience.

The bound strands of sound inside began to separate from an insensible gabble into individual voices. Nash recognized the voice of the Mexican he'd met outside Vardy's office earlier, he was losing, badly, and every other word he uttered was a cuss. Eight were talking around the table, but that didn't mean there weren't more, watching, silently.

Satisfied, Nash made his way quietly into the barn, found what he wanted and returned with a coil of rope. Tying one end to the post, and running low to the ground, he stretched the rope tight three inches above the top of the first step. Low enough not to be seen in the dark, and high enough to catch an unwary boot. Securing the end of the rope out of sight, Nash returned to the barn.

The inside was dark and warm from the horses stabled in there. He'd already found the one he wanted and led it slowly from the barn. Mounting bareback he rode the buckskin round from the barn and urged her on past the ranch house, pulling her to a halt he dropped down behind her, smoothing a hand down her neck to calm her.

The noise of her hooves on the hard ground had not been missed. He could hear voices inside raised in complaint and a moment later the door to the ranch house was flung open.

Nash had been expecting it, his face pressed against the horse's flank to preserve his night sight.

"It a goddam horse that's got out of the barn," one of Vardy's men complained, he stepped forward, Nash could hear the spurs rattling on his boots. "An' it ain't mine, so I ain't goin'."

"If you want a hand back in this game, Jed, you'll damn well go and get it," it was the Mexican who spoke, his voice loud and carrying across the yard to where Nash stood behind the horse. The mare shifted on the spot, tossing her head, Nash pulled a small, dried piece of oats laced with peppermint from his vest and held it before the horse's nose. The scent was so sweet the horse stopped and began snuffling his hand.

Jed grumbling, headed towards the steps. "I dunno why I gotta ..."

He didn't finish, his right boot caught under the rope, and he was pitched headfirst down the half-dozen steps. His senses dulled by liquor, he didn't save himself and his head cracked viciously off the bottom step, the first impact produced a thin scream, and the second nothing.

The light from the door was lost as men leapt up to see what had happened.

"That whiskey's seen to him, look?" One of them said laughing, pointing at the limp dark figure at the bottom of the steps.

The Mexican cussing, arrived. "Jed? Jed? Get your damned arse up."

There was no reply.

"Go on, Patty, you go and get that horse and give him a good kick on yer way past," the Mexican commanded, already turning and stepping back inside the ranch house, slamming the door behind him.

A second unfortunate headed for the steps, a shout of surprise splitting the night as he too fell headlong down the steps. He didn't knock himself out, the unconscious Jed saved him from that.

Nash fired from beneath the horse's neck twice. Patty was pushing himself up, one hand on Jed's back, another on the bottom step when the bullet caught him under the chin. It lifted him in the air for a moment, his arms suddenly flung wide before he collapsed forward on top of Jed.

The second hit Jed, the lead buried into his skull, he wouldn't be regaining consciousness.

Nash gave the buckskin a slap on her rump to send her away from the yard, and then unseen, in the dark running low, headed back towards the barn.

Inside Vardy's house.

Just after the plate of food was laid before her two gunshots rang out. Lucy jumped, her right arm hitting the table and making the cutlery rattle. "I'm sorry, sir. My nerves are not as good as they used to be."

"Dang it. It'll be the boys shootin' after coyote's, you've nothing to worry about, ma'am," Vardy said, attempting a smile which turned out to be more of a leer.

Lucy forced herself to pick at the meal. If it was well cooked, if the meat was tender, she couldn't have told you, her mind was fixed on Nash and the gunshots she'd heard.

Vardy's plate was clean. He'd wolfed down the meal like a hungry dog using his fingers to clear the plate. Grease splats had made their way onto the front of his shirt and more glistened on his chin.

Back outside.

Nash, out of sight round the end of the barn, checked his guns. He could hear the noise of confusion in the ranch house. Men's voices, cussed, boots pounded the wooden boards as they buckled on gun belts. Nash smiled.

The door to the ranch house was open, Nash could avoid looking directly at it, peering round the edge he had just the veranda in view. Wondering, his pieces ready, whether the dim-witted men in the ranch house would .... Nash didn't get to finish that thought, another of Vardy's men, his gun in his hand darted from the door and was immediately propelled into mid-air. The lead from Nash's gun went clean through him, entering mid-way up his ribcage and exiting in a sudden puff of red. He'd not expected to catch three with the rope – Nash smiled.

Back inside Vardy's house.

"Mr Vardy, that was mighty fine fayre, since my husband passed, I've not had much of an appetite," Lucy said, wanting to bring the meal to an end. "Can we talk about my husband's claim?"

"I like that in a woman, straight down to business, me and you are going to get along just fine," Vardy said grinning and displaying the stumps of rotten teeth that decorated his lower gums. "Now your husband, God rest his soul, had quite a claim. What were you going to do with it?" Vardy asked.

"I'd thought to ...." Lucy stopped as another sudden gunshot split the silence of the evening. Lucy jumped again, her foot banging the table leg making the plates rattle and one of the candle holders rocked precariously. "I'm sorry, Mr Vardy."

Vardy scowled. His hands on the edge of the table he hefted himself up. "I'll have this stopped."

Vardy lumbered towards the door and hauled it open. "Carter, where the hell are you?"

"Here, sir, Mr Vardy," came the instant reply.

"What the hell are those boys doin' out there? If Jed's drunk again and tryin' to shoot the weather cock I'll string him up, do you hear?" Vardy's voice was angry. "Don't just stand there, go and find out what's going on, damn you."

Vardy closed the door and returned to the table, when he sat down his weight made the chair creak in complaint.

Lucy smiled weakly. "You didn't have to stop your boys having fun on my account."

Half a dozen shots in rapid succession sounded from outside the house.

"God damn it!" Vardy cussed.

Back outside.

As soon as Nash had fired, he moved. Knowing the flash from his gun would have given away his position in the dark. At least six shots planted themselves in the wood at the end of the barn where he'd been stood or whizzed by thudding into the dried ground, one ricocheted off something metallic issuing a high-pitched squeal. A moment later the sound came back towards the ranch, echoing from the Oatman hills sounding like the drone of distant thunder.

The next noise was from the back of the barn, the sound of wood smacking hard on the ground, and the rattle as it came to rest.

"Round the back of the barn!" One of Vardy's men shouted.

Footsteps could be heard across the yard.

As Nash watched he saw them rounding both corners of the barn, converging on where the noise had come from.

"The bastards on the roof, must be," it was the Mexican standing over the ladder Nash had pushed to fall from where he had propped it against the roof. The men all pressed up against the barn wall knowing they were out of firing range from anyone above them.

Nash closed his eyes and listened.

"Goddammit, Luis, I'm not going up," one said. There was the sound of a sudden scuffle. "Jeez, Luis, there's no need to push that gun in my face!"

"Get up that ladder," the Mexican growled.

From where they were the men hauled the toppled ladder towards them and hoisted it once more against the side of the barn.

"What's goin' on?" A voice called across the yard. "Mr Vardy ain't right pleased with the noise you boys are makin'"

"It ain't us, Carter, there's a shooter on the roof, we got him trapped up there. Reckon he was after the horses, Pedro is goin' up there," the Mexican called back.

"Keep it down, Mr Vardy's a temper on him tonight," the reply from near the house came.

The Mexican's nominated man was already making a slow ascent, his left hand on the ladder his right holding a gun. Below him his companions held guns ready pointed towards the roof. Nash circled the barn bringing him to a thick wooden post where he crouched down.

"I can't see nothin', boss," the man on the ladder called down.

"Course you can't, you idiot, get up the ladder further," the Mexican ordered.

The man moved slowly, his feet rising two more rungs up the ladder. As he put his weight on the last one and pushed himself upwards his body became a visible silhouette against the night sky.

Nash fired. Just once.

They were all looking upwards to where Pedro was on the ladder and missed the flash from his gun. Pedro issued a guttural scream, dropped his gun but still clung to the ladder with his left hand. The impact of the bullet lifted man and ladder away from the wall, he was vertical for a second his right arm wheeling in the air, before he fell backwards landing with a sickening crump in the yard.

There was a moment of stunned silence. Then the group broke, two headed round to the barn entrance and the other two ran round the barn in the opposite direction.

Nash needed to take them both out if he was to keep his position unknown to the rest of them.

Believing their foe was on the roof they were running down the side of the barn, close to the wall.

Nash stood. Levelled the colt and fired, when the front man went down, he fired a second time. The bullet found it's mark in the man's left shoulder, he staggered.

Nash cursed. Held his breath, fired again and watched the man's gun fly up in the air as it was released from his dead hand. Gunshots rang out from inside the barn, the other two appeared to be firing indiscriminately upwards through the roof.

Inside the house.

Lucy reached for a glass of wine. She needed to do something with her hands which were shaking. "I'm sorry, Mr Vardy."

"No need, ma'am," Vardy said, but his good humor had evaporated. His voice was cold and grated through his rotten teeth. "So, you were thinkin' of selling, is that right?"

"I was," Lucy raised the glass to her lips, but didn't drink.

Vardy sat back hard in his chair. Two more bullets rang out from the yard, but he appeared not to have noticed them. "What I think, is that you stop here in Oatman, let me handle that claim for you. I'm sure it'll be profitable."

"Stop here ... I'm not sure what you mean," Lucy said, replacing the wine glass carefully on the table.

"Exactly that," Vardy waved an arm around the room. "It's a fine house, it needs a lady, and I think that could be you. I'll take care of that claim for you, don't you worry about that."

Lucy stared open-mouthed at Vardy. His hand had slid down to his crotch, and he was massaging himself through his pants.

Vardy stood up, his hand cupping his crotch, then he shouted towards the door, "Carter, get in here."

Back outside.

Carter had gone back inside the house; the Mexican had followed. Nash rounded the open end of the barn. Two quick shots finished the two men who were pointlessly trying to fire at the man on the roof. Running on light feet, keeping to the shadows, he headed to the house.

A long shadow, cast by the moon, of a man fell across the path before him. Nash instinctively dropped to one knee and the bullet the Mexican had fired went over his head. He couldn't see the man in the shadows. Sending two rounds in quick succession he heard the second hit, and the man grunted before falling to his knees and pitching forward away from the shadows.

Nash didn't stop. Inside the house was Vardy – and Lucy.

There was a door at the side of the house – it stood open.

Nash, his back to the wall, moved towards it slowly, both his hands holding the colts, ready. When he reached the frame, he stopped.

Somewhere in the house a plate crashed to the floor.

Nash tightened his hold on the guns and rolled his back around the doorframe quickly. Both barrels came to rest on a terrified negro, who was stood in the kitchen a cloth in one hand and a glass in the other.

"Don't drop it," Nash warned and raised both barrels towards the ceiling.

With a shaking hand the man put the glass on the kitchen table.

"Which way?" Nash asked.

The man didn't speak, but he raised a hand pointed at another door in the corner of the kitchen and then pointed towards the left.

Nash nodded.

Holstering a gun, he opened the door with his left hand, waiting for a moment before stepping into the corridor and letting the door swing closed against his boot, avoiding it rattling in the frame.

A higher pitched smash echoed along the corridor, followed by a choked cry.

Nash pulled the gun from the left holster and followed the noise.

"Hold her still! You're gonna wish you'd accepted my offer now!" It was Vardy's voice he could hear through the door.

Nash didn't wait. A boot squarely on the door he kicked hard, the catch gave way, and the door swung open, banging on a cabinet filled with glasses. The room was instantly silent apart from the delicate chinking as the glasses settled themselves squarely back on their bases.

Carter had hold of Lucy, a filthy gloved hand across her mouth and his other arm wrapped around her waist.

Lucy, her eyes wide, stared at Nash.

Vardy, his pants in a heap on the floor behind him, butt naked and with his cock in his hand stared incredulously at the man who had just dared to walk through his door.

"Let her go," Nash addressed Carter.

Rather than let her go, the man increased his hold on Lucy.

"Shoot him," Vardy instructed, waving his free hand towards Nash.

Nash didn't wait, the gun in his right hand fired. The noise in the small room deafening, acrid smoke filled the void between them and Lucy felt the hold on her release. A second later Nash was at her side.

"Stand behind me, ma'am. Vardy and I have a few words we need to have," Nash said, his voice cold, and his eyes never leaving Vardy's.

"My men'll cut you down like corn, son," Vardy spat back.

Nash shook his head. "I don't think so. You can try hollering' for them if you want, but they'll not come running anymore."

"Luis? Luis get in here," Vardy yelled.

His shout went unanswered.

"You're alone Vardy. I had a mind it was your boys who went after the women in Oatman, it wasn't was it. It was you?" Nash said, disgust in his voice.

"That shouldn't bother you. I'm sure your daddy planted his seed on an Injun girl after a few whiskeys," Vardy said, laughing.

Nash swallowed the reply he had been about to make. Nash was only trying to rile him.

"Vardy, Mrs. Murphy is taking her claim," Nash announced, then waved his hand around the room. "And all of this. A good woman needs a good home to live in."

Vardy laughed.

"Glad it's amusing you," Nash replied.

"And how, son, are you going to do that?" Vardy still sounded amused.

"You are going to make a gift of it," Nash said, he knew Vardy was playing for time, and as it happened, he didn't mind – Nash was as well.

Vardy pointed towards his pants on the floor and said with sarcasm. "You let a draught in, would you mind?"

"I would mind. You can just stand there like that," then to Lucy. "I'm sorry, ma'am, that you've to witness this."

There was a noise outside and Vardy grinned. Nash had heard the approaching horses already, but his expression didn't alter. There was the sound of men dismounting, then a moment later, solid boots on the wooden floor of the house as men approached down the corridor. A moment later Sheriff Wainwright opened the door and stepped into the room, a grim expression on his face.

"Wainwright, get this shit out of here," Vardy growled pointing towards Nash. "But leave the woman."

"Sheriff Wainwright, Vardy just tried to force himself on this poor widow, Mrs. Murphy, I happened by just in time. Seems he's a taste for it from what he's being saying," Nash spoke calmly to the sheriff.

Two of the sheriff's men appeared behind him, he turned to them, and they exchanged quiet words. The sheriff licked his lips, and refusing to look at Vardy said. "Take him boys, and for God's sake get him to put his pants on."

Vardy looked wildly between Nash and the sheriff. "Wainwright, you can't do this! I'll get the boys on to you."

At that the sheriff did look up. "Your boys are laid out there in the dust, Vardy."

"What did you tell him?" Vardy's eyes were wide with alarm, and he turned on Nash.

"I just gave him the opportunity to do what's right," Nash said, his cold blue eyes on Vardy. I'm much obliged, sheriff."

"That's not a ...." The sheriff never got to finish.

The sound of claws on the wooden floor was followed a second later by a grey fur head, with a flopped broken ear that appeared between the sheriff's men.

The dog's eyes scanned the room, took in where Nash's guns were pointed and he jumped, the rope around his neck trailing behind him. Even Nash winced. The dog had sunk his teeth into Vardy, but he hadn't gone for the throat, his target was much lower.

# EPILOGUE

Vardy didn't last long. There was a sort of trial conducted by Sherrif Wainright, which had had the sole purpose of allowing all those aggrieved by Vardy to say their piece. After that he was strung up from the hanging tree on the edge of town. He arrived on the back of a wagon drawn by two horses and had to be held up to have the rope dropped around his neck. He couldn't stand straight on account of the injury the dog had inflicted. It was said later by Doc Jerrod that Vardy was better off being hanged than to have lived given what the dog had done to him.

Lucy persuaded Nash to move into the house with her, but she couldn't get him interested in the claim. Gold was something the white man pursued; the shiny metal held no appeal to Nash.

Nash was sitting on the veranda at Vardy's house, his eyes on the beauty of the sun as it set painting the sky in a breathtaking array of colors, deep oranges and fiery reds to soft pinks and gentle purples. The sun descending towards the horizon casting a warm golden glow that bathed the landscape in light. The clouds, catching the last of the sun's rays shimmered like gold. The silhouettes of the mountains providing a stunning backdrop, enhancing the beauty of the scene. He knew the plains were calling him.

Nash felt the gentle pressure from Lucy's hand on his shoulder and a moment later a glass of whiskey appeared before him. Nash took it, and Lucy lowered herself into his lap, wrapping her arms around his neck.

"It's beautiful," she said, then after a pause she asked. "Will you stay?"

Nash sipped at the whiskey, then turned his eyes away from the distant scene towards her face. "It's tugging at my soul, Lucy, I cannot lie to you," Nash finished the whiskey and abandoned the glass on the veranda, "But believe me now you're tugging at my heart more."

Cupping her face in his hands his lips met hers as the light from the day faded.

The End

Next in the Series

The Gunfighter's Law

Printed in Great Britain
by Amazon

49237006R00108